HALTER-BROKE

Also by John Reese

SURE SHOT SHAPIRO
THE LOOTERS
SUNBLIND RAGE
PITY US ALL
SINGALEE
HORSES, HONOR AND WOMEN
JESUS ON HORSEBACK: THE MOONEY COUNTY SAGA
ANGEL RANGE
THE BLOWHOLERS
THE LANDBARON
THE BIG HITCH
SPRINGFIELD 45-70
WEAPON HEAVY
THEY DON'T SHOOT COWARDS
THE SHARPSHOOTER
TEXAS GOLD
A SHERIFF FOR ALL THE PEOPLE
BLACKSNAKE MAN
SEQUOIA SHOOTOUT

HALTER-BROKE

JOHN REESE

DOUBLEDAY & COMPANY, INC.

GARDEN CITY, NEW YORK

1977

All of the characters in this book are fictitious, and any resemblance to actual persons, living or dead, is purely coincidental.

ISBN: 0-385-12820-7
Library of Congress Catalog Card Number 76-55680

Copyright © 1977 by John Reese
All Rights Reserved
Printed in the United States of America
First Edition

For Mildred Peterson, just because it's a delight to know her.

HALTER-BROKE

CHAPTER ONE

A dozen trees, their trunks polished brightly by the sensuous rubbing of itching cattle and their leaves now turned red and golden by early frost, stood on top of a low, round hill. The two men circled to keep the trees between themselves and the naked valley where the rich, tough bluestem grass so far had resisted the frost. Nearing the top, they dismounted, with the midafternoon sun of early September at their backs.

"You ain't going to believe this, Alec," said Mose Henry. "I've heard of Indians walking down wild horses, ain't you?"

"Yes," Alec Pitman grunted.

"How about a white man? Or boy, ruther, because I swear that's all he is, a snot-nose boy."

They led their horses warily into the trees, ready to grasp nostrils and shut off any sound the horses might make to give away their presence. Alec Pitman's heart gave a giant leap as Mose Henry said, "Lucky us. There he is in plain sight. Ever see anything like that?"

"No," said Alec.

Nearly half a mile away, close to where a line of trees marked Buford Creek, a lean, gawky, ragged kid who could have been anywhere from twelve to twenty, stood as still as a statue, watching a dapple-gray filly from some fifteen or twenty feet away. The filly was watching him.

There they stood, just looking each other over without fear.

Alec took the short brass spyglass from his pocket and handed his reins to Mose. The glass had so small a field of focus that it was almost useless from the saddle, but he was skilled with it. He extended the short tube and held his breath until he had brought the boy into sharp focus.

"What's he look like up close?" Mose breathed.

"He's sure a ragged-ass varmint. Bet he ain't had a haircut for nigh a year. Or a bath either."

"Tracks show his moccasins is about wore out."

"Filly's only a bangtail," Alec said, shifting the glass to the horse. "About two, I reckon, and never will make a set of legs. It beats me how people go stone blind to a horse's faults when it's a gray. I wouldn't own that miserable cull."

"You don't. That's a Bar X horse."

"I don't see no brand on her."

"No, but I seen it around since it was borned, and a Bar X mare dropped it. That kid has been follering it for weeks. You see his sign everywhere."

"Why wasn't I told?"

"What was there to tell?"

"Why, this is my land, you idiot," Alec said.

He realized, too late, that he had let himself in for an argument. All you had to do was give Mose Henry an opening.

"There's quite a few squirrels in them trees that we never told you about either, Alec," Mose said. "I see the mail rider every now and then, and I ain't never once bothered to report that. I missed something, somehow, Alec. I just never figgered that an expedition of one ragged kid and one stray bangtail was a danger to you, and I'm sorry."

"Oh, shut up," said Alec, "and watch this."

His chest filled with a combination of many feelings—admiration, envy, excitement, suspense, and a touch of bitterness as he saw the kid saunter toward the worthless gray filly. He was going at it exactly right. He was pretending that he didn't see the horse and the horse didn't see him. He acted as though he had all the time in the world, and was going to be mighty surprised when he looked around and here was a horse.

Eventually he got to where there was no more than a couple of feet between his flat, empty belly and the gray's head. Then he looked at her, but he did not move. It was as though he was saying, "Well hey there, horse, what are you doing here? Anyway it sure is nice to know you."

"Making her make the first move," Alec said, softly.

"Onliest way to handle a horse or a woman," said Mose. "They can't neither one stand being ignored by you."

The filly put her head out to have her ears scratched, and the kid scratched them. His hand strayed along her short, unkempt mane and dropped over her neck. She came closer to let him lean against her to reach down and scratch her throat. Alec could feel how good it felt to both of them—better than anything he had ever got out of life himself, it seemed now.

"If he had himself a rope," said Mose, "he'd have himself a horse now."

"Reckon he would," Alec sighed.

"Beats all. Just picked her out and walked her down, but now what the hell's he going to do?"

"How does he live?" Alec asked.

"Will and Tango claim they've heard gunfire. I reckon he hunts his provender. How else would he get it?"

"But nobody ever saw him before?"

"Not until I seen him today. You know what I think?"

"No, what do you think?"

"I think he had to take the chances of being seen, to finally come up to her. I think he's holed up down there along the creek, but he had to show himself today because this is the end of his chase—or it would be if he had a rope. If you ask me, Alec, he's wilder than the damn horse."

"But you don't *know* where he camps?"

"No, but I bet if you searched Buford Creek, you'd find it somewhere close, because this is where the filly waters. She's used to him now, don't you see? She gets lonesome for him when she don't see him."

Alec said, softly, "Yes, now she needs him as much as he needs her. People talk about a smart horse—hell, there's no such thing! It's all habit. Teach them a thing, get them used to it, and that's what they want all the rest of their lives. A wild horse likes being wild because he's always been wild. Get him used to a fenced lot and feeding from a crib, and that's what he wants. That's why all it takes to walk down a wild horse is time. Time to get used to you."

"My daddy," said Mose, "used to say that only a human man has the power to decide things. An animal does what he has always did, but a man can think things out and change."

"Well," said Alec, "some can, I reckon."

A fifty-year-old look settled over his face. Alec Pitman was a man of average height thirty long, hard years old, with good shoulders and thick arms and legs that gave him a look of strength and endurance. With more rations and less hard work, he might have been called chunky.

But a money-making single man who was responsible for an irresponsible mother carried a burden that thinned him down over the years. A fourteen-hour working day was about normal for Alec. He had brownish hair that Ma kept whacked short, brown eyes, a good chin, a good set of teeth. There was a little bit of a strut in his walk that said to get the hell out of his way, he was taking the short cut because he was busy.

Yet you could pass him in any crowd and not notice him, mostly because of his work-worn look. Nesters had the same look, like next year was the year they'd give up completely, they just couldn't stand any more. Yet Alec Pitman was half-owner of the Broken T, his mother owning the other half.

Mose Henry was the nearest thing to a foreman that Alec would tolerate. Mose was bigger than Alec, stronger, better-read, and better able to say what he had on his mind. That could be a nuisance, but you could forgive a man his big mouth if he turned in the kind of day's work that you got from Mose. Whatever you told him to do, you could forget it, it would be done.

Mose would never amount to anything because he lacked the inner drive that made Alec rich—and miserable. Mose was about forty, and he had all he wanted out of life—good job where they set a good table, a few dollars in his kick most of the time, and a small crew to drive and bully and talk to. Talk and talk and talk to.

"Hey, look," said Mose.

The kid had slid slowly along the horse, keeping his weight against her. He put both arms across her back and stood on tiptoe to let part of his weight go on her. The filly ignored him at first, but when he gave a little spring with his tiptoes and let all of his weight go on her, she sidestepped impatiently.

But she did not run and the kid did not try to force the issue. He just leaned against her again, to the infinite pleasure of both, it looked to Alec.

"He's done that before," he said. "Soon he'll straddle her, and slide off before she can throw him. Keep doing that until before she knows it, he's riding her. Then in a week, he'll have her answering to his weight like he had a saddle and bridle on her."

"Like an Indian," Mose agreed, nodding. "I told you, he's wilder than the horse is."

"Yes," said Alec, "and let me tell you something else, Mose. There's the best horseman you ever seen in your life. There's the kid I'd like to have working with me this winter, gentling colts that we ain't going to have time to break for the market otherwise."

"Say, there's an idee!"

Mose flung himself into the saddle like a fool, and whacked his horse with his heels. "Let's put it up to him before he can get away," he bawled back over his shoulder.

It was too late to tell him to mind his own damn business. The wild filly knew the moment Mose rode out of the trees. She streaked away, and the kid was hard put to keep his feet. But he did. He ran too. Horse and kid both headed for the creek, one to the left and one to the right.

By the time the kid was in the trees, Alec had mounted and was spurring his horse after Mose. "Let him alone, you tarnation idiot!" he shouted. "Hold up there, Mose. Hold up, I say."

Mose reined in and turned, his face full of woe. "Now see there, you let him get away!" he wailed.

Alec hauled his horse in beside Mose. "Damn it to hell," he raged, "don't you ever stop to think? I ought to drive you into the ground like a stake."

"Why," Mose said, in that bellow he always used when he felt hurt or indignant or in the wrong, "you said you wanted to hire him. You know you said that!"

"I said I'd *like* to. If he wanted a job breaking somebody else's horses, do you think he'd be out here walking one down all summer?"

"But Alec, it's the biggest favor you could do him, you know that."

"Yes, but does he? Now look what you've done."

The kid came out of the trees, carrying a shotgun. He sprinted toward them and stopped suddenly to raise it to his shoulder.

Both men's instincts were honed sharp for moments like this. They had spun their horses and dug in the spurs before the kid fired. Even so, it was lucky that he was loaded with light bird shot instead of buck or BB. Both of their horses felt the sting, and Mose screamed like a panther when one hit the back of his bare neck.

But most of the pattern rattled harmlessly off their heavy fall jackets. They turned immediately and forced their skittish horses to stand. Alec's was still feeling the sting of bird shot against its rump even though none had penetrated.

"Damn whelp, damn ungrateful tramp," Mose quavered, rubbing the back of his neck.

"Serves you right. Nobody likes somebody to sneak up on him that way," Alec said. He stood up in the stirrups and waved his hat. "Hey, kid," he shouted.

The kid, without answering, turned and loped back toward the creek. He did not seem to be trying to run hard, but he was covering a lot of distance and not taking much time to do it. His legs, Alec thought, just had to be like spring steel. Like an Indian's.

He disappeared like an Indian, too. One minute he was there, and the next there was not even a shadow flitting through the trees along Buford Creek.

"He's sure-enough camped around here somewhere," said Mose. "I'll bring a couple of the boys over here before dark, and smoke him out. Learn him to fire at me when I'm only doing him a favor!"

"No, you won't," said Alec. "He ain't doing no harm. What you're going to do, you go back to the place and get a couple of pieces of old rope, enough to make him a stakerope and a hackamore and an Indian jawline. That's all he needs for that horse."

"*What?*"

"You heard me. I want that boy to have that horse, and he is not to be bothered on my range, not no way! Just don't get yourself shot, is all."

"If he shoots at me again," said Mose, "there'll be a forty-five hole through him in some mighty personal places, I gor'ntee him that."

"You just lose the rope, that's all, and don't fool around. Wave your hat to show no hard feelings, just in case he's watching somewhere."

"Which he will be."

"And then get the hell out of there for home."

"Why, Alec? Just tell me why!"

"I just want to see if he can get a rope on that miserable bangtail. If that's what he wants, he's entitled to her and I mean for him to have her."

"But she ain't yours to give," said Mose. "I told you, damn it, she was dropped by a Bar X mare. You could maybe make a deal with Buck Buchert, but since he's let Dave Conn take over running the Bar X—"

"I'll hand Dave a ten-spot and he'll forget to hand it on to Buck, and that's nine dollars more than that horse is worth."

"Not if they don't want to take it. A man still prices his own horse in the good old U.S. of A."

"No, go by Paul Trotter's place and pick up a piece of rope there. It's closer than home."

Mose threw his leg over his saddle horn and got ready to make a long, sociable afternoon of it. "I see. And what'll you be doing while I'm losing a rope for this worthless wild kid to catch his worthless wild horse with?"

"Tell Ma I may be home for supper and I may not. I'll fry myself some eggs if I have to, tell her."

"What'll I tell your ma if she asks if you have went to see the Widow Butterworth?"

"Goddamn it," said Alec, "just tell her that you don't know and it's none of your business where I went. For once in your life, just do as you're told."

Mose patted the neatly coiled rope at his own horse's side. "This rope of mine," he said, "is about played out. It's going to bust on me one of these days, and somebody's going to have his lap full of a six-hundred-pound steer. How's about I—?"

"All right, all right," said Alec, almost at the end of his temper. "Lose that one and stop and get a length of hardtwist from Paul, and get home and make yourself useful."

"Well," said Mose, "your ma is going to ask if you went to see Mrs. Butterworth, and you know me, I can't look her in the face and lie to her. So if that's where you're going—"

But Alec had turned his horse and was pushing it south by east. He was still on his own range, but if he held this course he'd cross a worthless corner of gullied range owned by old Buck Buchert and being run for him—badly —by Dave Conn. Alec Pitman was a man who did not bother to have enemies, but if he had had one, Dave would have been it.

And if he kept on just a couple of miles, he'd be in old homestead country where everybody had gone broke and a fellow by the name of Lance Butterworth had tried to buy up all those old claims and make himself a cattle ranch. He died before he could finish the job, leaving a widow who simply did not give a damn if anybody gossiped about her. Or if everybody did.

Well, Mose said to himself, taking the rope from his saddle, I have did the best I could to keep old stupid Alec out of trouble. . . . Now all he had to do was lose this rope where that kid could find it and then go get himself a new hard-twist from Trotter. Time to buy himself a five-cent bag of hard candy, and sit and jaw with Paul and Reva, and still get home for supper.

CHAPTER TWO

Mose's skin tingled a little as he approached the creek, but in his heart he did not really fear the kid and his shotgun. He reckoned Alec had the kid ciphered about right. Alec was usually right, and the kid probably just wanted to be let alone, was all.

He found himself a nice, round rock that stuck up out of the bluestem, and laid the rope on it. He sat his horse there long enough to smoke a couple of cigarettes. He picked up the rope a couple of times and then put it back on the rock.

When he rode away, he was pretty sure the kid would know the rope was there. If he hadn't been watching somewhere from the shelter of the trees, Mose just didn't know human nature. He felt surer than ever that he was right when he saw the gray filly feeding just beyond the creek. She'd stick pretty close to the boy, for sure.

His duty done, and smartly, too, he put his horse to a canter, looking forward to a visit with Paul and Reva and catching up on everything that had happened lately. When you ran a crossroads store and blacksmith shop and made a weekly freight trip to the U.P., wasn't much that missed you. Whereas if you worked for somebody like Alec Pitman, you couldn't be sure what color the house was painted because you left for work before daybreak and didn't get back until night fell again.

There was a wide wagon road west of here that ran straight to Trotter's place, and shortly after Mose Henry struck it, he saw two big brown horses feeding along the roadside. "Now, what the hell!" he said aloud. He rode closer, to make sure of what he was already sure of in his mind.

Yes, that was Duke and Dolly, Paul Trotter's freight team, half Belgian and half bronco. And what were they doing out here? Paul never let his team run loose.

Mose got behind them and whooped them on their way. They did not want to go home, and he regretted having left his rope on the rock. What they needed was to have their butts stung with the knot of it. Old big-footed, clumsy, stubborn elephants liked being free now. But wait until winter, and see how they liked it.

Mose liked old Paul Trotter. He even liked Reva Trotter, and not many did. The blacksmith had opened his shop when there was only a crossing of trails. He did good work and made money from the first. Soon he built a little store building and looked around for somebody to run it for him. Why he chose Joe and Reva Bliss, nobody ever understood. They were just riffraff that Paul picked up in Cheyenne, and probably took pity on.

All this was before Mose Henry's time. Joe Bliss got drunk and froze to death the first winter they were there, and the next summer, Paul married the widow. Reva ran the store, but she was a lewd, foulmouthed, surly old woman who would have been more at home running a cathouse. She sure didn't attract the family trade.

Mose pushed the team down the road, one horse in each wheel rut, and the closer they got to home, the less they wanted to go there. In the grove of trees in which Trotter's Corner, as they now called it, was located, Mose saw Paul's chickens and one hog. That didn't seem right, either. None of Paul Trotter's stuff ran loose.

It struck him that things were just too silent. No dogs barking, no ring of hammer on anvil, not even a hen cackling. When he came into sight of the place, and Duke and Dolly made another break to get past him, he saw why, and let the horses go free.

Paul's fine split-rail corral was down. So was his hogpen fence. The doors to the smithy and store stood open. Something, Mose knew, was dad-blamed wrong here. Real wrong.

For some reason, he felt nervous sweat all over him as he got down and tied his horse to a sapling about a hundred yards from the big, well-built store building. The living quarters were attached to the rear. The smithy stood in a separate building beside it. It hit him then:

The chickens were going in and out of the open door of the store. He took his .45 out and spun the cylinder. He carried it in his hand as he approached the buildings.

The first thing he saw was a dead dog, the big, woolly one that Paul called Brutus. No question about how it died. Brutus had been shot through the mouth, the slug going up into his brain. No question in Mose's mind as to how that had happened, either. The dog had been jumping at someone on horseback, and whoever it was just let him jump and caught him at the top of his leap, with his mouth open.

There was another dead dog, the little one that Paul called Feisty, closer to the house. Mose, feeling clammy all over, and not ashamed to admit to himself that he was scared stiff, faded back against a tree and, with his back to it and the gun in his hand, thought it over. Looked things over, too.

Paul was a master builder. To pull his corral fence rails down, you'd have to snub your rope around the saddle horn of a good horse. Same way with the fence around his hogpen. The chicken yard would be easier. You could just kick it to pieces, and that was what it looked like someone had done.

Oh lordy, Mose thought, oh lordy, lordy, lordy! What'll I do? Well, the first thing is look inside. . . . What he really wanted to do was jump back into the saddle and get out of here and pretend he had never been here.

The silence was the terrifying thing. For all Mose knew, somebody could be lying in ambush for him anywhere. Except, that is, for one thing. There was no horse in sight anywhere, and whoever had done this to Paul and Reva was not going to wait around here afoot.

He forced himself to go into the door of the store. It was not a big store but it held a lot of stuff. There were a couple of hens on the counter. They enraged him so much that he snatched his hat off with his left hand and swiped it at them.

"Shoo," he said, "shoo! Get the hell out of here."

One went his way and past him out the door. The other went the other direction, behind the counter. He leaned over the counter to take another swipe at it, saw Mrs. Trotter on the floor, and had to sprint for the door to throw up. He barely made it.

He did not have to go back to see if Reva was still alive. She wasn't. He went around to the smithy and looked through its open door. No sign of anyone there. He went to the back door of the house part of the store building, dreading to find it open. It was open, all right. He cocked the gun and, sweating harder than ever, stepped through it.

He was in the big kitchen where they ate and sat to read of an evening, both Paul and Reva being readers. Or had been. Not much to see here, except that someone had sure filled up here and left the dishes. Fed like a hog, in fact, two of them. Big double loin of venison, baked with potatoes but just hacked to pieces. Almost a whole blackberry pie.

That, Mose told himself, kind of tells me the time, yesterday noon. . . . Reva, whatever else you could say about her, was a first-rate cook. The venison roast was done, ready to eat. Mose touched it and then the stove and found both cold. They ate their big meal in the middle of the day, but they had not had a chance to eat this one.

Say about eleven-thirty yesterday, the grub ready to eat but not eaten. Say twenty-eight hours ago, if that was any help.

Gun cocked and held in a steady hand ahead of him, Mose went into the bedroom and again wanted to throw up. Paul had been tied to the bed and treated something awful. He had suffered a lot before somebody just plain lost patience with him and shot him in the belly, below the heart, so he would live and suffer a little longer. The bedroom was just absolutely torn to pieces.

Mose knew what had happened as surely as if he had been there. Always there had been talk that Paul Trotter made more money than he spent, and that he had some of it hidden around somewhere. Plenty of it.

Well, a couple of drifting cowboys had tried to make him tell where it was by torturing him. That was easy to see. Had to be cowboys because only they would know how to pull those fences down so efficiently. They'd have tied old Paul up and spent a few minutes wrecking his place and turning his livestock out, just to show him what they could do if he insisted on making trouble.

And then, Mose decided when he went through the door into the store, probably Reva had got gay with them. Called them a few choice names, and she sure had some choice ones at her command. Where they made their mistake was in killing her. It looked to Mose as though someone had put a .45 against her temple and just let her have it.

What did Paul have to lose after that? They sure didn't know him if they thought torture would get anything out of him, once his wife was dead. She might have been an old battle-ax, but she was Paul's battle-ax and he had taken pride in taking good care of her.

Mose stepped around Reva's body and went out the front door, shooing more chickens out of the store and closing the door behind him. Immediately he found the tracks of shod horses. Now, Mose Henry did not claim to be any Indian when it came to reading sign, but any fool could see that there had been *two* shod horses well trained to the rope. And *two* hardcases who would do anything for money except work for it.

He forced himself to look things over closely. Here were the marks of old Paul's boots, no doubt where he had been tied to a small tree with his arms behind him while they tore his place to hell. You could almost hear them: "All right, old man, how do you like it? We got plenty of time. When we get done wrecking your place, we start on you."

A butchering hog, a barrow that would weigh two and a quarter and would go to close to three hundred by January, had been shot in the back. Again, someone leaning out of the saddle had taken that shot. The hog had died hard in the edge of Reva's young apple orchard, and there went half of the winter's meat.

Where they made their mistake was in killing Reva. Mose was one who believed, with good reason, that old Paul *did* have money stashed away around here. Now it would probably stay hidden forever. Paul would die—and had died—rather than tell where it was, and no one else was going to find it.

"Why," Mose asked aloud, unable to get the squeak out of his voice by clearing his throat, "didn't they just set the place afire? Old Paul had twenty years—no, at least twenty-two or three—years of work in this. Burning him out would break his old fool heart."

He knew the answer to that almost before he had it asked. A column of smoke would have gone up that would be visible for miles. People didn't drop into Paul and Reva's place every day, but those two bastards had had more than their share of luck to spend as much time raising hell here as they had without somebody blundering in. Smoke would have brought somebody sure. You could even have seen the smoke from the Broken T.

What should he do?

Well, one thing, run the damn chickens out and close the doors, but leave everything else for the sheriff to see. Not that he would do anything but run around in circles and worry about what this was going to do to him at the next election. Sheriff Max Maddox, with two x's in his name, was a cinch to be called Double Cross behind his back, and he was. Not so much crooked as dumb. Promise somebody something and five minutes later promise the same thing to somebody else.

Long old ride into town, though, and Mose's horse was already tired. Thing to do was head for Buck Buchert's

Bar X and swap horses. Maybe let Dave Conn send one of his men in to get the sheriff.

No, that wouldn't do either. Max would want to know about it from Mose Henry. "God damn the luck!" Mose moaned, as he climbed into the saddle and headed for the Bar X as hard as he could push his horse. "I don't go around looking for trouble. Why did it have to be me to find them?"

At the Bar X, no one was home but Buck. He was oh, fifty-four or five, a pleasant, spineless little old nobody whose worst vice was that he just couldn't say "no." Hard worker in his day, when his wife was alive to tell him what to do. Now it was Dave Conn who told him, to the point where you couldn't tell who worked for who.

"My heavens, that's awful," Buck said. "Take the bay mare. Too bad Little Si ain't here, but Dave is giving him a workout today. Oh, what an awful thing to happen! Who could it possibly be?"

Mose switched saddles, leaving his horse in the smallest corral. Old Buck threw it some hay as he talked. "Country's full of no-goods this time of year," he went on, answering his own question. "My heavens, some of the riffraff you see getting off of the freight trains, it makes you wish the railroad had never come through."

Buck claimed to be able to remember back to when there was no U.P. He was a native, had been born right in this very house. Had been to Omaha once, but nowhere else. Buck would be perfectly content to sit on his shoulder blades with his feet up under a tree he had planted himself, and let somebody bring a bowl of beans to him three times a day.

"Wasn't no train bums done this," Mose said. "What old dumb Max wants to do, he wants to look around and find who just laid off a couple of hands that rode horses shod all around. Onliest way he'll ever pick up the sign of these two."

"My heavens," Buck said again.

Mose mounted the bay mare, feeling less than heroic as he faced the prospect of breaking bad news to Sheriff Maddox. "Thanks, Buck," he said. "Keep your eye out for a couple of hardcases mounted on shod horses. Shoot first and ask them who they are when they can't answer, that's my advice."

The bay mare rode like a camel, but she could cover the ground. She was in heat, and flighty as an old maid at a box supper, and she didn't neck-rein the way a good cow horse should. Dave Conn couldn't do anything right. Every horse that Alec Pitman owned was taught to handle right, and if it couldn't be taught it got a good selling.

Which brought up the subject of horsebreaking, which reminded Mose of that wild kid who had walked down the gray filly. What if *he* had killed Paul and Reva? Mighty strange, him turning up and them finding Paul and Reva murdered the same day.

Impossible. The kid wore moccasins, not boots, and he had no shod horse, else why would he be making a lifetime job of walking down the gray? Best not to mention the kid to Max. He'd turn out a posse to run him down, and waste a lot of time asking him dumb questions, while the real murderers—two of them—got farther and farther away, and safer and safer from retribution.

CHAPTER THREE

Alec Pitman's daddy used to say that he got the blues every autumn, because each one might be his last one. Finally one was. Reed Pitman had suffered enough to last several men a lifetime, but complaining about the fall of the year was the only bellyaching Alec had ever heard him do.

Reed had been a captain in an Iowa regiment when he was wounded and captured in 1862. He was in several hospitals and prison camps before he ended up in the hellhole of Andersonville. He had gone into the Army as a kid. He came out of Andersonville an old, broken man.

But not a bitter one. He enjoyed life. "Alec," he used to say, "you may not have the Puritan conscience, but you've sure got the Puritan need to suffer. For a little tad, you sure are a worrier about things you can't do anything about anyway."

It had taken him two years to get the farm in Iowa back into shape, cripping around on two staffs and trying to get a day's work out of the restless ex-soldiers who were all you could hire then. He couldn't wait to get married. The girl he chose was a moody, pretty, harebrained neighbor girl of fourteen, by the name of Edie Burke. But a grown woman in everything but good sense.

Right away she got pregnant. "I'm sick of Iowa," she

said. "This is no place to bring up a child. It's too crowded. Let's sell the farm and move west, Reed."

"Well, why not?" said her husband, cheerfully, although he had dreamed of Iowa all through the war and had never considered living anywhere else. "Where would you like to move to?"

"Wyoming," said Edie. "That missionary that was staying with the Knebels told me about it. It's wonderful! Let's move there and you go into the cow business."

Wyoming it was. Alec was born before they could get rid of the farm—at a good price—but he could not remember Iowa. His earliest memories were of watching his father age as he learned the open-range cattle business. Just when he had it mastered, barbwire and homesteaders caught up with him.

Reed Pitman had bought the Broken T when it was a little old shirttail spread with a one-room log house in the foothills on the edge of five thousand owned acres. By the time he died, when Alec was almost sixteen, he had bought up all the grassland near him, had more cattle that he could handle profitably, and had added six rooms to the original log house.

He had also added to his debts. Paying those debts was what had made Alec look old at thirty. Well, now they were paid, and he and his mother were joint tenants in fee simple in a very fine cattle property. They had a bunkhouse on the place now, too, but Edie still cooked for the hands and fed them from the big family kitchen. She had a broken-down old cowboy to help her, but she was a worker.

She had remarried a couple of years after Reed Pitman's death, fellow by the name of Amos Shook. That didn't last long, only the name. That was typical of Ma's judgment. She and Amos went to Cheyenne to get married, parted at the door of the post office, and had never seen each other since.

So it galled painfully when the hired help asked Alec, "You sure this is what Miz Shook wants? It ain't what she said the other day."

She wore the name of Shook as a penance. Alec never bothered to answer them, and they knew better than to ask a second time. But it still galled.

All right, he thought, cantering his horse through the deep grass that usually made him feel so good, so well prepared for anything that could happen, I'm a rich man, and what do I get out of it? Nothing . . . He had started out the day with the blues, and seeing that wild kid had made it worse. He was a prisoner, that was what he was, same as his daddy had been at Andersonville. Hell.

He let a fence down by pulling a couple of staples, holding them in his mouth as he stepped his horse over the bottom wire. He used the same heavy fence pliers that had drawn the staples to drive them back in again once he had crossed.

Now he was on Buck Buchert's Bar X range, a long triangle or peninsula of which stuck out like a sore thumb between Alec's Broken T and Mrs. Butterworth's place. And soon, this time without having to worry about a fence, he was on the Widow Butterworth's sorry little Four Plus.

Her husband, whose name, so help him God, had been Lancelot, had had a pretty good idea. A lot of homesteaders had proved up before going broke, and he had bought them out and let their farms go back to grass. This just wasn't wheat country.

Only trouble was, Lance had started too late and then

had not lasted long enough, dying just when he could look forward to making a little money in a few years. His widow was bound and determined to do it alone, and Dave Conn was bound and determined to help her.

Esther Butterworth was what Alec wanted more than everything else in the world. She was the only woman he had ever felt that way about, the only woman he ever expected to think of in connection with the word "love." He knew that she and Lance had not been happy together. He thought he could be the man to make her happy and that Dave Conn could only make her miserable.

But there was Ma. She did not like Mrs. Butterworth and she was not going to have *any* woman sharing her house and that was that. *Her* house, by God!

A U.P. train whistled distantly—or not so distantly, after all. The country changed radically here. Lance had tried timothy and grama grass on several of these old homesteads, and had even dug up sods of bluestem to transplant. He had the right idea, yes, but he started too late. To get pasture growing again, you had to rest it, and anybody as hard-up as Mrs. Butterworth had to feed off everything that grew.

The Four Plus brand looked like 4+, only Butterworth had made it so small that you had to get close enough to smell the critter's breath before you could identify one of hers. Butterworth hadn't believed in hurting a beef more than necessary and he called big brands cruel. He had been just an opinionated fool.

Alec stood up in the stirrups. That finger of Bar X land, all of this Four Plus land, and some more of this ratty, abandoned homestead land belonged by rights to the Broken T. The natural boundaries of the Broken T could not be ignored, any more than any other natural boundary. It was dead wrong for Buck Buchert and Esther Butterworth to bleed these odds and ends of grassland to death to no purpose. But try to reason with them.

Sometimes, Alec thought, sitting down in the saddle again, I wonder whether it's the woman or her property I want most. . . . Well, there was no question about that, really. He wished she'd *give* the damn Four Plus away and marry him, before that greedy, ambitious son of a bitch of a Dave Conn got her and the Four Plus and the Bar X and everything in sight.

How, Alec asked himself, could I stand it if she'd have him? I'd want to kill him, I reckon. . . . And if he couldn't have her, what Alec wanted to do now was to walk out. Just that. Put a handful of raisins in his jacket pocket, a couple of hundred bucks in his poke, and head for nowhere. Not walk down a wild horse because the kid had beat him to that. But something.

But there was Ma, Edie Shook, who had only the third decree of divorce ever granted in Wyoming. Still wild-eyed and moody, still thought she knew more about everything than anybody on earth, and not afraid to let you know it. And she did not like Esther Butterworth.

It was little enough Ma got out of life because being rich had done her no more good than it had Alec. That was why he could even forgive her Amos Shook, married in haste and repented after a divorce in leisure. Poor damn woman, he couldn't abandon her.

The Four Plus came suddenly into sight, a nice four-room frame house with a big sheep barn that now held a hundred tons of bluestem hay. Chicken houses so tight a weasel couldn't get in. Hogpens. Pens for bucket-fed calves. It ain't a ranch, he thought disgustedly, it's a damn farm. . . .

There was a big heap of fresh dirt about forty feet from the back door. Just then Esther came to the door and opened it, and put her hand on her hip as she recognized him. He straightened up and gave her a salute and heeled his horse into a trot.

Lance Butterworth had been against an orchard, but she had started one after his death. Alec tied to one of her three-year-old apple trees and walked toward her, taking off his hat.

"Oh," he said, stopping beside the heap of dirt and the hole from which it had come, and taking off his hat, "digging you a new well?"

"It's new," she said, coming to him, "but I'm not sure it's a well yet. So far it's just a hole in the ground."

He recognized the windlass over the shaft with a griping pang of jealousy. It was Buck Buchert's, and old Buck sure wasn't digging anybody's well. No, Dave Conn was doing this, while he ran Buck's Bar X into bankruptcy by mismanagement and neglect.

It was a good windlass, eighty feet of one-inch rope on the spool and a wooden bucket that held almost a quarter of a yard. You could put down a lot of hole with this outfit, and it was like new.

He leaned over and looked down. Nice, straight hole, forty inches in diameter and about twenty feet deep without a sign of water. Then Mrs. Butterworth moved so close to him that he started to choke. It seemed he could smell her nice clean hair and some other kind of flowery soap smell.

"What do you think?" she asked. "Is it a well or just a hole in the ground?"

"There's plenty of water down there," he replied, "but

it may not be easy to reach with a dug well. On the other hand, maybe you can."

"You're not much help, Alec."

He leaned over and fingered some of the dirt from the hole. "It's gritty to the touch. Could be you're near water-bearing sand. I'll tell you how it is with a well here. Up where I am, every well has to be drilled at least a hundred feet, but most of them come in artesian. South of you a few miles, down near the tracks, you can drive a sandpoint down ten feet and never pump it dry.

"Here, you're right on the boundary, you might say. It could go either way. Your old well's a dug well, ain't it?"

"Yes, dug ten feet down and then bored with an eight-inch posthole auger for another fifteen or sixteen, and tiled with plain old clay tile. There's water there, but it's so far from the house and it doesn't take long to pump out an eight-inch hole."

"Well," he said, swallowing as he met her eyes, "there's your answer. You'll hit water soon."

"Oh, I do pray to God you're right!"

"I take it Dave Conn has been digging this for you. How much is he charging you?"

"Every foot, and he won't take a cent."

"Who cranks the windlass?"

"I do."

Now her eyes were sparkling with amusement. No question about it, she enjoyed having both him and Dave running after her, seeing who could do the most work on the Four Plus for her. You couldn't blame her any more than you could Ma, but she just couldn't see that you did not dare play games with a son of a bitch like Dave Conn.

Esther was about Alec's age, maybe a little older, but she didn't look it. She came from New York and there was

Iroquois blood on both sides of her, Mohawk on her father's side, Seneca on her mother's. Her maiden name Tappaw, was supposed to come from some damn Mohawk word.

A tall woman, almost able to meet his eyes at his level. Skin that tanned nicely with freckles that came through darker still. Black eyes and hair, but the hair was too wavy to have come from the Iroquois. Big, warm-looking, soft-looking mouth that made him just absolutely lustful.

She covered her face with her hands, turned pink through the tan, and looked at him between her fingers. "You're looking at my freckles," she said, "I know, aren't you? I get them from Grandma O'Neill and my big feet and hands from Grandpa Patton. But I think my figure is mostly Indian, don't you?"

That was the way she was, deliberately say a thing like that, daring him to look at her fine, large bosom and flat belly and wide hips. Sometimes she put on pants and a man's shirt and worked like a man. Rode better than most men and could rope a little if she had to.

It was torture for Alec to ride beside her and try not to see the bouncy-bouncy-bouncy of her bosom, and she damn well knew it and let it bounce. What drove him crazy was thinking of Dave Conn looking at her the same way, the filthy-minded son of a bitch.

"How," he said, dropping his eyes to the hole in the ground again, "are you going to case it?"

"That's my next worry," she said. "I've got the money for the brick. It's waiting behind the U.P. depot in town. Just what Dave said to order, curvature on a twenty-inch radius. Does that mean anything to you?"

"That's right," he said.

"But Dave says when he hits water, it's more than a

two-man job to keep it pumped out while he cases it, and I've still got to get the brick hauled out."

He scratched his jaw now, wishing he had shaved today, although why he should have he could not see. "Suppose," he said, "I bring a crew over here and gopher out the rest of your well and send a couple of wagons in for your brick. We can have you a cased well in a couple of days, way that bottom grit looks to me."

"Do you think that's fair to Dave?"

"Fair? Why ain't it? What's fair got to do with it?"

"Oh, Alec, for God's sake, this is something Dave wanted to do for me. I haven't seen hide nor hair of you for a month. Now just when Dave is close to water, you want to come in here with your big gang of men and rob him of the gift and the credit."

He could only stare at her. "Credit? Hell, let him have the credit. What you want is a well, ain't it?"

"You don't even realize what an overbearing bully you are, do you? Just when Dave has most of the dreary, thankless work done—oh, it's so typical of you, so much like a rich man!"

Finally he got it and could stop strangling. "All right, let Dave bring in your well, let him case it while you pump it out, let's don't hurt his Goddamn feelings whatever we do! Why don't you hire a man to help him?"

"Who? Help is so high, and you should see what comes around, looking for jobs as haying hands. I keep Robber and Wolf in the house every night now. For the first time in my life, I'm uneasy about being alone."

Alec almost said that he was willing to bet that Dave had made good friends of her watchdogs, Robber and Wolf, but he remembered he was not supposed to hurt Dave's feelings. "Forget about the hay," he choked. "I'll send a crew over and get that in for you. That won't make Dave cry, will it?"

"Oh, if only you could do it on shares!" she cried. "You can always use more hay, can't you?"

He wondered how you dug a well on shares, and what Dave figured to get out of it. "I've got all the hay I can feed up for the next two years, Esther. Move some of your fence and get them fattened up for the January or February market. Raise some cash before those culls eat you out of house and home."

"Dave says hang onto every critter I own."

He rolled his eyes hopelessly. "Jesus Christ, what does he know about it? Some of those scrubs of yours shouldn't be allowed to breed. You figger on it. I'll stack your hay here and you get your cows this side of the fences, and I'll come over here about January and cull out a couple of carloads for you."

"What would they be worth?"

"About half of what you'll get, that time of year. Say, Sixty head at twenty a head, less shipping charges to Omaha—say you net out a thousand dollars."

Tears filled her eyes. "Oh, if I only could! And use the money to buy better cattle. I know, you're right, and Dave isn't much of a stockman."

At least she had that much sense, but it became pretty clear that she wasn't going to ask him in for a cup of coffee and a piece of pie. He mumbled that he had to be getting back home, if there was nothing he could help her with long as he was here.

"You could help me carry out a tub of water and dump it," she said.

"Sure."

She led the way into the house, where he noticed that

the kitchen curtains were drawn. The tub was in the middle of the floor, and the room reeked of that same flowery scent. She had been taking a bath, that was what, and he went suddenly weak at the thought. Just weak as a cat, discombobulated because she'd let him help empty the water.

They each grabbed a handle and carried the tub outside. "Let's dump it down the hole," he said. "Soften the dirt and make it easier for Dave to dig."

She was not sure he was serious until he had led her all the way to the unfinished well. He tipped the tub and let the water go.

"That just never occurred to me," she said. "My first thought would have been that it would contaminate the well. But that's ridiculous, isn't it?"

"Yes," he said, and their eyes met and held like a half-inch cable, and he wondered what she was thinking, and just did not have the guts to ask.

"What are you doing in this neck of the woods?" she asked.

"Backtracking a wild kid that's been walking down a wild two-year-old filly."

"*What?*"

He explained about the kid. "I thought that was what you said," she said, "but I never heard of it being done. There's something splendid about it, isn't there?"

"There sure is, but don't tell Dave about it. It's Buck's horse. Now, look. If you need help on this well, Esther, and Dave's tender feelings will let him, tell him to send over for a couple of men. I'll stay away and just send him a couple, how's that?"

"Alec, you know as well as I do that I wouldn't dare

mention your name to Dave. Come on, I'll walk you to your horse."

He ached so much to touch her that he offered her his hand, and she took it and they walked along like a couple of kids coming home from school. He untied the horse and then could not bring himself to leave.

"I see so little of you lately," she said. "How's your mother?"

"Fine as frog's hair," he said. "Everything I say seems to rub you the wrong way lately, Esther. Seems like I'm always in the wrong, and a man hates to always be saying he's sorry."

"I guess it's mostly my fault," she replied, lifelessly. "I'm probably getting moony, being alone so much. I wouldn't trade places with anybody, but it gets so *damn* lonesome sometimes."

There was his chance and he dared not take it. He fitted a boot carefully into his stirrup and rose up into the saddle.

"Ought to come spend a couple of days with Ma before the snow flies," he said.

"Now, Alec, you know I'm not welcome there."

"But God, you are! It's half my place."

"Oh, you know what I mean!"

"I know that between Ma and Dave Conn, I can't call my soul my own any more."

"I've never seen the inside of your house. My nearest woman neighbor, and we barely speak when we meet in town. Oh, listen! Does she read much? I've got lots of books I'd be glad to let her read."

Esther had taught high school someplace in Nebraska, whereas Alec had never even gone to high school. It was a long time since Ma had read a book, although she used to read all the time. The truth was, Ma was scared Alec might marry someday—Esther or any woman—and she'd have a daughter-in-law in the house.

If Esther would have him, and Ma made trouble, she should be the one to get out. He felt that strongly, but something told him that Esther was not going to walk into a knock-down-drag-out fight like that. First you settled your other problems and then you could feel free to ask Esther. Sure, sure.

"Kind of you to ask," he said, "and I'll see if she wouldn't like something to read."

"She won't."

Again their eyes met. "You know," he said boldly, "people are the damnedest fools! Not just Ma and Dave. Me and you, too. Whatever the tune that's played, it's easier to dance to it than say it ain't your style."

She quoted to him:

"'And the muttering grew to a grumbling,
And the grumbling grew to a mighty rumbling;
And out of the houses the rats came tumbling.'"

"What's that? I've heard it," he said.
"From 'The Pied Piper of Hamelin,' by Browning."
"I remember Ma reading that to me when I was a little bit of a kid, and it's sure the truth. Why do Ma and Dave have to run my life for me? Why can't we both do the neighborly thing, you and me, and you come over and stay with Ma a few days while I help Dave finish your well?"

"Because when the piper pipes, you dance too. I just wonder where you were a month and a half ago, when Dave offered to dig my well. I'll tell you where you were.

Home, because your mother wouldn't like it if you hung around down at this end of the Broken T."

"Well," he said, "you never busted your butt to be neighborly either, Esther. I'm proud and you're proud and Ma and Dave take advantage of us. If I asked you to marry me, what would you say?"

"I'd say provide a house of my own for me or come live here in mine."

"There you are."

He touched his hat to her and let his horse head for home, and yet could not free himself of the spell of her. Not just her body, which heated him like a prairie fire, but something suggesting a companionship the like of which he had never felt in his life. Something like sitting beside a stove together in the wintertime, not a word said, but missing nothing on God's earth either because she was there. Something about being proud of her, trusting her wherever she went, because there was an armor of propriety and decency about her that would take some living up to.

But which left her with a blind side, too, because there wouldn't be any propriety or decency about Dave Conn, or any respect for them either, the damned guttersnipe. Whether Esther knew it or not, Dave could not be trusted, the no-good son of a bitch.

Alec knew cattlemen who wouldn't do a tap of work with their feet on the ground. It was the damnedest thing, how they drew a line between saddle work and hard manual labor. *They* did the roping because they owned the outfit. The cheap help did the branding and earmarking and cutting, and even though they all ate from the same tin dishes at the chuck-wagon tailgate that evening, it was still two different classes of men.

Alec Pitman had never understood that way of looking at things. It seemed to him that any man whose pride depended on being in the saddle was in bad shape. What if he lost his saddle? No, if a man really had any pride in himself, he carried it on him no matter what he did.

Alec loved nothing better than digging. He liked to get out and spade up his mother's garden patch each spring. He loved to dig postholes and set posts and string wire— and not just to make his crew whimper to keep up with him, as Mose Henry said.

No, he just liked the work. When he thought of being down there in the bottom of Esther's well, digging for her, with her up there turning the windlass, it was like a gas pain under his heart. He could have dug by himself, something Dave couldn't do. Fill the bucket and then shin up the rope hand-over-hand to raise it and dump it, and do it all day.

He had proved that, digging the waste hole for the water closet Ma had made him buy a few years ago. She had read about them somewhere, and sent off to Philadelphia for a catalogue, and had one shipped out so she wouldn't have to go out to the privy like common, ordinary people. Only trouble was, in the winter, when you needed it most, it didn't work. The water tank Alec had had to set on stilts behind the house froze over, and the only privately owned water closet in Wyoming was out of business until the spring thaw.

But you couldn't ask saddle hands to dig a waste hole, even if it was just a clean hole in the ground while you were digging it, any more than you could expect them to dig a new privy hole and help move the privy. You hired

Doc Docherty for that, because that was his trade, the way he made his living. You respected him the same as everybody else did, because he was a specialist, sort of.

Anyway Alec had dug the damn waste hole himself, twenty feet deep and forty inches across, and walled it with the same bricks Esther Butterworth would use for her well, because seepage out *and* seepage in were the same thing to a set of bricks. Did a mighty good job of it, too. Old mouthy Mose said next thing you knew, Alec would be selling and installing water closets all over Wyoming, and driving Doc Docherty out of business.

How had he got to thinking of privy holes, anyway? Why, because that was the way a man's pride was, if he was a man afoot or horseback. Which wasn't the kind Dave Conn had. He only hoped that Esther realized that. You wouldn't catch Dave digging a hole for a privy. But the things he *would* do, Alec was sure, proved him scum of the earth.

Maybe Esther did understand. At least she had waited until Dave was gone, and still had pulled the kitchen curtains shut, before taking her bath.

CHAPTER FOUR

Buford Creek was fed by a series of springs, but runoff rainwater had washed a channel big enough for a river. "This time of year," the kid grumbled to himself, "it's real nice, all right. But come the spring freshets, and I had better be gone from here."

He watched Mose Henry stage his opera with the rope, leaving it at last on the rock, and then retreated to the cave he had enlarged under the soapstone overhang in the clump of red oaks. The oaks' roots had been pretty well exposed by floodwater on the one side, but they had roots enough on the other to survive many another spring flood. The kid had gophered out under them until he had a cavern, really, about ten or twelve feet square and almost high enough to stand up in.

He had dug it with an old shovel picked up in a junk pile when he was skulking around the crossroads blacksmith shop last spring, right after he spotted the gray filly. He had known then—instantly, and for the first time in his life—why he had been born. He remembered hearing about Indians "walking down" a wild horse. He had no idea what it involved or how it was done, only that he had to do it. What he was looking for, when he found the shovel, was something to eat.

He had dug a little side chute to bring fresh water into his dugout, as he called it, and carry it out again. He had an armload of hay for a pillow and an old blanket for a bed. He had gone into town 'way last spring and laid in some supplies of ammunition and grub, before his money ran out, and he still had some cans of tomatoes and almost a gallon of syrup left. He had lived mostly on meat. Flour gone, meal gone, salt gone, coffee gone.

And now, ammunition too. He had fired his last shell at those two cowboys this afternoon. Now he might have to see if he could walk down a deer, too. He was pretty sure not. Have to kill a calf, or learn to trap rabbits. How did you trap a rabbit, anyway?

He waited until almost dark before coming out of the shelter of the trees. He sprinted to the rock and snatched up the rope. He took a quick look around, in all directions, before sprinting back to the shelter of the trees. He knew he could outrun any man alive in these parts, on foot. He did not know how he knew it, but he knew.

He was not afraid of those two cowboys. If they had wanted to run him down, they could have done it. It seemed to him instead that they had respected his right to be alone.

What terrified him was the memory of those two men who had camped for two nights farther down the creek, but not much farther. He first learned about them when Jewel betrayed a strange sort of nervousness and refused to let him come within a country mile of her. That was the name he had given the gray filly, Jewel.

Jewel was getting to where she seemed to feel about him the same way he felt about her, but she still did not trust other human beings. Like today, when those two cowboys showed up. She had taken off like a deer.

The other day she had just kept on running. She had

never done that before, and it bothered him. He had squatted in the shelter of the trees until almost dark, and then had slipped down the creek to find out what it was that had spooked her.

It was not hard to find. They were so close that it infuriated him as an act of trespass, if he had been able to think of it in those terms. They had a little fire going, but a very little one. He easily got close enough to find out why it was so small.

They were drunk, that was why. They had been drunk for a week. They were sobering up now because they had no more to drink and no money to buy it with. They were both old grandpa fellas, at least forty-five or fifty years old. Real old, anyway, and real bummish. In a few minutes he could tell them apart.

One was called Haze, for Hazelwood, Bill Hazelwood. He wore a pretty good coat, but everything else he had on was ragbag. He had a toothache that he had been carrying for a month, and it was that that had started him to drinking. Kind of a short man, pretty bald when he took his hat off although his hair grew long over his neck and ears. Yellow hair turning gray.

The other one was Ezra Tully. Ezra talked like a New Englander, and the kid sure knew how a New Englander talked. He said "pa't" for "part" and "cows" for both "cause" and "course," and "da-naow" for "don't know." Both of them badly needed shaves, Ezra worse because his whiskers were dark and were not graying with any particular attractiveness.

And say, were they in a peck of trouble! That pleased the kid, only why did they have to bring their dang troubles here? This was his place! He resented even their staked horses, out in the deep grass. He sat and listened and hated their guts for quite a while.

"Haze," said Ezra, in that twang of his, "get some more wood and build up the fire before it goes out."

"Jesus," said Haze, "you must be crazy. I told you, the least move and I think my head is going to bust with this Goddamn rotten tooth."

"I offered to stab it and dreen it for you. There's a pus pocket in it. That's what it needs, to be dreened."

"It needs to be pulled out."

"Here, let me feel it. Maybe it can be pulled out by my fingers. Hold still a minute."

Haze held still a minute and then let out a shriek of agony. Ezra yelled too.

"You like to bit my thumb off," Ezra said. "It's so loose it's like to fall out. Just let me get a good, strong grip on it—"

"The hell with that. You ain't a doctor."

"I know what I know. Here, let me cut into the side of your gum and dreen that shit out, Haze."

"You put that Goddamn knife away," Haze shouted, leaping backward despite his pain. "Go fetch some wood yourself."

"I'm not the one that's cold. I'm not the one that's got the pus pocket in my jaw. I was only thinking of your comfort, Haze."

"Oh, sure you was."

"Well, I was. I don't think we ought to have a fire here anyway. What if somebody saw it?"

Haze fell into a shivering, weeping fit, but Ezra showed him no mercy.

"Hell of a partner you are," he said. "If you was half a man, we'd be rich as goose grease right this minute. I bet that old booger has got a thousand dollars hid away. Maybe two thousand. But you didn't have the guts. *I* have to suffer because *you* have no guts."

"I've got guts," Haze said, weeping, "but I hurt so bad with this tooth, I couldn't do it. That's the God's truth, Ezra, I wasn't up to it. I was a sick man."

"What makes you think you'll be well tomorrow? I'll tell you this, Haze, either we clean out that old blacksmith man, or you and me is through."

"I'll be all right tomorrow."

A long silence except for Haze's weeping. Then, slowly, Ezra got to his knees, stealthily, silently, so Haze did not take alarm and look up.

He jumped suddenly, sprawling all over Haze and knocking him flat. The kid felt like screaming when he saw the long-bladed knife in Ezra's hand.

"You sure are going to be all right tomorrow," Ezra drawled, "or you're going to be dead. Either I cut into that gum and take that tooth of yours out, or I cut your Goddamn throat, and I don't much care which it is."

Haze tried to scream, but all he could do was gag and wail. He gave up quickly and stiffened his whole body to stand the pain of the knife. He opened his mouth, with Ezra sitting astride his chest, holding the knife in his right hand. With his left thumb, he probed inside Haze's mouth.

"Eh there, Bill Hazelwood, if you ain't the biggest baby in the world!" he said. "The pus pocket broke. Turn your head and spit it out."

Haze gagged and wept and spat.

"No, sir," Ezra said, "that tooth is about to fall out, and I mean to have it out and get you in shape for a job of work tomorrow. Open your mouth again."

Pleading sounds from Haze.

"Open your mouth," said Ezra, "or I mean it, by God, I'll cut your throat."

Down came the knife—slowly, slowly, slowly. The kid got silently to his feet and ran, making no sound because he was used to running through the dark by now. The skin all over his body seemed to be wanting to shiver with horror. He did *not* want to be there when a man got his throat cut. Oh no!

He dived into his dugout and sat there wishing he had something to eat. Later, the fit of fear passed enough for him to crawl out and climb up to the top of the creek bank again. He saw a faraway twinkle that meant that the fire had been built up again.

Curiosity was greater than fear. He slipped up close to the fire again, and it did not take long. Haze was the man feeding it, but he was unable to talk. He felt better, that was clear, but he surely had one sore old jaw on him.

"You ain't hurt," Ezra was saying. "I just got the point of the blade under her and tipped her out, like shelling a peanut. Haze, you are just worthless, that's all. You can't fish and you can't cut bait, you can't bake what you eat or brew what you drink, you're just useless. But you're going to be of some help to me tomorrow, by God I vow, or this time tomorrow night you'll be laying there in the woods with your throat cut. I don't know how I ever came to be partners with the likes of you, but now that I am, you're going to pull your oar. So you build up that fire and keep it burning and—oh Christ, I wish I had a drink! I *need* a drink. And it's your fault, Haze, you son of a bitch, that I haven't got one."

The kid did not sleep that night, not a wink. He was

sitting with his head barely above the creek bank when they led their horses down to the water in the morning, and then saddled them. Haze was at least able to saddle his own and mount without assistance; so Ezra's crude surgery had been effective.

Oh, what a pair of bummers they were! They'd be real mean this morning. Hungry, cold, sleepless, hung over—oh, say! They sloshed across the creek, both grabbing at their saddle horns like ladies to hang on, they were in such bad shape, and headed north.

The kid had never been more than a quarter of a mile north of here. He and Jewel were both at home, and at ease with each other, south of the creek. It was a huge relief to the kid to see the backs of those two, and it seemed to please Jewel, too.

For in less than an hour after the two went out of sight, here she came, trotting so smartly that it was almost a prance and shooting her ears forward to look for him. She was so durned pretty that she made the kid want to cry, and she let him come straight to her and whack her on the shoulders and under the belly like a tame old barn horse.

Today was the day he could have put a rope on her, no question about that, but he did not want to and he knew why. Those two bummers, Haze and Ezra, had sort of stunk up everything. This beautiful, beautiful gray horse was—well, kind of holy to the kid. That was it, holy. So holy he could come right out and say it aloud, "I love you, Jewel, like I never loved any other thing on this earth."

Jewel tossed her beautiful head and snatched up a mouthful of grass. The kid leaned against her, with one arm across her back, and crossed his legs. She was carrying a good bit of his weight this way and she seemed to like it. But this was not the day to put a rope on her, not after those two had stunk everything up around here.

CHAPTER FIVE

Bullheadedly, Alec took the shortest short cut home, a deep penetration of Bar X range that he had forbidden himself for the last couple of years. Mighty lean range, too. He shook his head at the signs of overgrazing that he saw everywhere. Dave would have poor old Buck in the poorhouse in a few more years.

Not that Buck was that old, but he just was not a hustler, and he had turned the Bar X over to the worst share manager he could have found. It was too bad. Dave told it around everywhere that he wasn't taking wages, that if he didn't make the Bar X pay he was just wasting his time. But what he was fixing to do, it was clear to Alec, was take over the whole place someday and leave Buck not much more than a cook and flunky on his own property.

He came within a mile and a half of the Bar X, which once had been a pretty good-looking place. At least it had been neat and well kept. Alec wanted to come no closer. What it had become in the last couple of years would be sad to see.

It was his bad luck to run into Dave, who seemed to be heading for home. Dave was riding the only decent horse that Buck owned, a little bay stud that he called Little Si. The stallion was nine years old, but as tough as he had ever been, and gentle as a kitten. He got the best cutting horses in the country, and Buck should have been breeding him to his own mares and raising himself a good cash crop of cutting horses instead of standing Little Si to other men's mares.

The two men hauled in their horses civilly enough, but there surely was no love lost between them and never had been. "Kind of strayed off your main-line tracks, haven't you?" Dave said.

"Little bit, maybe," Alec replied. "Got your hay all in?"

"Didn't cut much this year."

"How come you didn't?"

"Didn't have the crop, that's why. We grazed off some of the hay meadows. But we got plenty of stacks to see us through the winter."

Yes, Alec thought, but how about the next winter, and the one after that? It was an offense against nature to abuse range by running too many scrubs that should have been culled out last spring. . . .

"Tell Buck if he thinks he's going to run short, come over and team some of my baled hay to your place," he said.

"Alec, we just can't afford it."

"'We' your hind end, Alec thought. . . . "If there's one thing I've got too much of," he said, "it's hay, and Buck would do the same for me. Now that's Gospel, so you tell him to help himself."

"Where you been?" Dave asked suddenly, his mind darting off business and lighting like a deer fly on the thing that was riding him like a witch.

"Four Plus," Alec said.

"See Mrs. Butterworth?"

"Why, yes I did, Dave, if it's any of your business."

"What did you want to see her about?"

Dave did not raise his voice, made no threatening move, did not so much as narrow his eyes, yet Alec sensed that he had gone over some kind of an edge. Dave's decent streak had always been pretty narrow—invisible when he lost his temper—but he had always had sense enough to know there were some things one man did not say to another unless he was deliberately courting trouble.

Once again, Alec wondered how it would come out if it came to a fight between them. Dave was maybe an inch shorter, but at least thirty pounds heavier. They were about the same age. Well-digging would shape a man up, and he sure had no belly on him. Hard as a rock, he looked like.

Usually it was hard to make out Dave Conn's face for the tangle of black, curly beard on it and the wild berry-patch of black, curly hair he wore. But since Alec had last seen him, Dave had had a short haircut and had mowed all the whiskers except a big, square, bristling black mustache. At least now you could see his eyes, and they were not worth waiting for. As blue as the glass vase Ma set so much store by, and just as blank and hard.

"You've got your gall with you, Dave, to ask me a question like that," said Alec. "What the hell business is it of yours why I wanted to see her?"

"I done made it my business, Alec. That's my woman and I warn you fair and square—stay away from her!"

"Dave," Alec said, disgustedly, "the fool-catcher is after you for sure. Suppose we both get down on the ground and you tell me that man to man."

Dave's face lighted up as though he had not dreamed he could be so lucky. He slid from Little Si's back and let the reins drop over the stud's head to the ground. Little Si would stand "ground-tied" until he starved to death, he was that well-broke a horse.

Alec dismounted more carefully. His gelding was scared of the stud. Alex kept its reins in his left hand. Dave came toward him with his right fist pulled back against his belly and his left out, like a man who had fought for a living. And he probably had.

"Hold it until I tie my horse," Alec said.

He wondered if Dave ever heard him. "All right," he said, "I'll tell you again, stay away from the Four Plus, you son of a bitch. She's my woman and I'll kill any man I catch flirting around there."

Alec said it again: "Let me tie my horse. He hasn't got a lick of sense."

Neither had Dave. Dave jumped him, jabbing with his left. He rapped Alec twice on the side of the head with it, and one thing was sure, he could hit like the kick of a mule. Alec knew he was not hurt, but he never had stood this kind of pain well. Couple of times, in kid fights, he had almost killed the other boy because he took a few that hurt.

Alec's horse shied, and Alec lost his grip on the reins. Alec had Dave all over him, left jabs and right hooks that would have had Alec out like a log had Dave not been in such an all-fired hurry. Alec simply lifted the .45 from his holster and jammed it into Dave's belly so hard Dave could not ignore it.

Dave looked down and saw the gun. "If you want to take your chances I won't shoot," Alec said, "go ahead." His lip stung. His mouth was full of his own blood, and he hated that as much as being hurt.

"You offered to fight me," said Dave, "and you pull a gun on me. Jesus Christ, you're a sport, you are."

"You didn't think I was going to stand here one-handed and try to hold my horse and let you beat the hell out of me, did you?"

"I dare you to pull the trigger."

"You don't have to dare me. Just make one Goddamn wrong move. Put your hands up and turn around."

Dave dared him for a split second, then up went his hands. Alec felt of him for a gun and found a .32 in his hip pocket. It was well oiled and every chamber was loaded. Alec stepped back with the .32 in his left hand, his own .45 in his right.

He stepped back three steps.

"Turn around," he said. "That's a sneaky way to pack a gun."

Dave turned around. "I ain't a rich man like you. That's all the gun I can afford."

"I've got a forty-five I can let you have, but wear it like a man. Now there's two things I want to get across to you, Dave. One, you don't tell me where I can go, ever. Two, don't use Mrs. Butterworth's name like that to me or anybody else. I'll kill you if you do."

Dave was white as a sheet, but he seemed to have decided that Alec meant it, and for once he was keeping his temper. He let his arms come down slowly, without waiting to be told he could.

"Alec," he said, "you think that just because you're a rich man you can have anything you want. Go ahead and shoot if that's your style, but I tell you once more, that's my woman and there ain't no amount of money on earth that can buy her."

The poor devil really believed it was that kind of a deal. Being rich put a man in a bad position lots of times, and this was one of them. Alec holstered the gun, but he made sure he kept his hand near it.

"Be reasonable, Dave," he said. "I went over there to be neighborly and offer to help her get in her hay. I seen where you was digging her a new well. That's right neighborly, too. That's a hell of a nice thing to do for her, with winter coming on and so much work of your own to do. I admire you for it."

Not one word of which was true, but a man got into a position where he had to lie like that sometimes. He doubted that Dave heard a word of it, however.

"You and your Goddamn money," Dave said. "You and your Goddamn Broken T. You got the law on your side, the banks, everything. But you ain't got her and you don't scare me!"

Again Alec tried to talk sense. "If any of that made any difference to a nice woman like Mrs. Butterworth, do you think I'd be standing here arguing with you? No, I'd take a posse out there and levy on her, same as I would somebody that owed me money."

"Oh, sure! All you have to do is snap your fingers, and everybody from the judge on down hops to it. Well, I don't!"

The man's head was pure granite. Alec gave up and pulled the gun out and let Dave see him thumb the hammer back.

"Now, *I'm* going to tell *you* something, and you're going to stand there and listen," he said. "Mrs. Butterworth is the only woman in the world for me. If she wants you instead, or some other man, or nobody—all right, all I want is for her to be happy. But I don't want her scared or hurt, and I don't want her embarrassed by your Goddamn crazy talk, and so help me God, Dave, if you make that kind of trouble for her, *I'll kill you.*"

"This don't end it," Dave said.

"I reckon not," Alec said wearily, "but it's all for today. You've made me lose my horse. I'm going to have to borrow yours because mine is headed for home. I'll send Little Si over to you tomorrow sometime."

"You'd put a man afoot?"

"You've got a mile and a half to hoof it and it's your own fault and it won't kill you. I'm going to keep your sneaky little pocket pistol, though. I ain't even going to shame you by telling where I got it."

Dave seemed to consider trying to scare Little Si into running, but he thought better of it, probably because the horse wouldn't run anyway. Alec mounted the little stud and turned him around. He had heard he was like a rocking chair to ride, and he sure was. There was no thrill on earth like being on a horse you knew was the absolute best. The kid who had walked down the gray filly would appreciate this one.

"Oh," Alec said, "another thing. Buck's got a mare that dropped a gray she-foal a couple of years ago."

"Yes, I know about her."

"How much does he want for the filly?"

"I don't know as she's for sale."

Alec grinned. "Dave we ain't going to get into no horse-trading game. A friend of mine taken a fancy to her because of her color. I told him she's hammer-headed and sheep-necked, her pasterns are too straight and she's pigeon-toed and narrow-chested and never will make a good set of legs. But he's just a kid and his heart is set on her, so I told him I'd offer Buck ten dollars for her."

"Ha!" said Dave. "Ten dollars. For that much, I might sell you her halter."

"What the hell you mean, she ain't even been halter-broke. How much?"

"Hundred dollars."

"Oh, your foot. Tell you what, you butcher her for meat this winter."

Alec realized that he had let Dave trap him into horse-trading after all, but you had to do these things.

"Hundred dollars is cheap for that horse, Alec."

"Oh, shoot," Alec said.

He started to ride away.

"Eighty?" Dave called after him.

He stopped Little Si and turned him. "I'll go as high as twenty so I must've lost my good sense."

"Come on, we've got some crips in the cull pen you couldn't buy for twenty. That's a rich man for you, make fun of what the poor man has and then try to beat him out of it."

"You've got crips because you've got bad horses to begin with and you don't take care of them. This kid is a plain fool about that gray, though, so tell you what I'll do, Dave. I'll go as high as fifty."

Alec again started to ride away. Little Si had the easiest trot he had ever ridden. Over his shoulder he saw Dave run after him.

"All right, then, fifty," Dave shouted, "if you've got the cash."

Alec stopped Little Si and turned him. "Stop right there," he said.

Dave stopped. Alec peeled off two twenties and a ten and felt cheap about flourishing so much cash money in front of a poor man, but damn it, what else could he do?

He nudged Little Si close enough to hand Dave the bills.

"I'll send somebody over with a bill of sale for Buck to sign in a day or two," he said. "Thanks, Dave. And I meant what I said—that's a nice thing you're doing, digging Mrs. Butterworth's well. But don't make no wild bets without you check your hole card first."

He headed for home. This Little Si was even better than his reputation when it came to sitting him, and Alec had already seen him work. How high would he have to go to buy the horse from Buck?

Again he felt cheap, flaunting his money to take the only decent thing Buck owned; but it was a cinch that somebody would catch Buck holding short and end up with the horse before spring. Yes, and not pay half as much as Alec, either.

I'll do it, Alec decided. Pay him twice what the horse would fetch from anyone else. I've got to own this fella. . . .

The thought made him feel good. When it came to him how that wild kid would whoop with joy when he heard that the gray filly was his, he felt even better. Mrs. Butterworth would probably call it "bullying," but he still felt better.

But he felt not quite so good when he remembered Dave Conn and that fifty dollars. Dave had been quick to demand cash. What the hell was his hurry? Alec took it for granted that Buck Buchert probably would never see a dollar of it, but he'd sign the bill of sale anyway like the old fool he was.

But what did Dave need with cash? Why did the idea of Dave building up a pocket wad and digging Esther's well at the same time make him suddenly uneasy? Alec had learned to respect his hunches. As his daddy had said, hunches were the seepage from a great reservoir of knowledge and inspiration that people didn't even know they had. In war and in military prisons, you learned the difference between a hunch and a guess. A hunch was the unborn truth, say about in the fifth month.

"And that," Reed Pitman had told Alec, "is one of the most profound truths I acquired as a graduate of Andersonville College. Be sure it's a hunch, not a hope or a guess, and march accordingly. When it's finally born you'll see you were right."

This was a hunch, for sure. All right, Alec would watch that scared, dishonest, ambitious, miserable fist-fighter like a hawk. No way to warn Esther, though. She'd take it as more bullying.

CHAPTER SIX

A man was entitled to a little luck on a day like this. Mose Henry had his when he overtook Sheriff Double Cross Maddox three miles from town. The old fool, just when he needed to be astride, was in a buggy pulled by a team Mose had never seen before. Like Alec said, you could put your hand under Max while he was on the nest clucking his head off, and you were a cinch to find fourteen doorknobs and one good egg.

"Hold up, hold up," Mose shouted, waving his arms as he pushed his tired horse across the open grass toward the road.

Max pulled in his team. They looked like steppers. The old fool had probably gone into debt for them just to make a big show campaigning from a buggy next election, and you could bet your Sunday hat that the people would pay for them.

"What the hell's the matter with you?" Max shouted, when Mose got close enough to hear him. "What do you mean, skeering my team?"

"Looks to me like you got a strong hand on them," said Mose, "and I hope to hell they can step because Paul and Reva Trotter has been murdered."

"Lordy, lordy," Max moaned. "Lordy, lordy, what next? Murdered? By who for Christ's sake? Are you sure?"

He just about went all to pieces, sitting there in his new buggy with his new team and hearing the news that could cost him the next election. Max was a big old hulk of a man, going to fat on the county payroll.

"Well," said Mose, "it sure ain't a case of self-destruction as forbidden in the Good Book. I seen the bodies. It's a horrible sight that would puke a dog off'n a government gut-wagon."

"How come you to see them?" Max asked suspiciously.

"Because I went there. Now ask me why I went there and I'll tell you it was on Alec's orders to buy myself a length of hard-twist rope for a new saddle rope."

"How'd you happen to need a new rope today of all days?"

Max could ask the dumbest questions. Mose knew that Alec would brain him with a two-by-four if he got that wild kid mixed up in this. Cunningly, he said, "Mine's been wore out for a long time and it busted today. Jesus Christ, do you want to tell me I committed these murders, you old fool? I beg to remind you that I ain't no drifting cowhand. I *live* here, I'm a *voter* in this county, besides Alec and his ma there's two *other* voters at the Broken T, and right there is five votes you're fixing to throw away. Not to mention a lot of people that was friends to Paul and Reva. Or Paul at least."

Max pulled himself together. He made a good speech and when he trimmed his beard and put on a clean shirt, he sure-enough looked like a sheriff. And now and then he acted like one. He began doing so now.

"Dad-blame it," he said, "I wish I had a good horse under me, but tie on behind and get in with me, and let's find out if this pair can run."

They could run, all right. Both Max and Mose almost

forgot the grim and sad purpose of the run, in their delight with the team. "I know they've got some bad habits," Max said, "but that don't bother me. Fred, the near horse, is a biter, and Jake will crowd you in the stall. But I'll break them of that."

"You can break a crowder by carrying a sharp stick to let him crowd against," said Mose, "but you ain't ever going to break a biting horse of biting."

"Bust him in the nose."

"That works that one time, but the next time he's still going to try to take a chunk out of your arm."

They argued that around while the team flew over the twin ruts, bringing them closer and closer to the horror of Trotter's Crossing, as Max called it. The new horses were not even winded when he pulled up in front of the store, a good hour before dark.

"You show me," he said in a trembling voice.

"I don't look forward to it one bit," said Mose, "but come on."

The sheriff had to step outside and throw up, too. "Such good people," he said, wiping the tears from his eyes with a wrist the size of a wagon tongue. "Who would do something like that to lovely people like Paul and Reva?"

This was how the old churn-brain kept getting elected, because he said things like that and meant them. Again Max pulled himself together.

"We've seen all we can see, all we need to see," he said, "and my God, we can't leave those poor bodies here all night again, Mose. Where's Paul's team?"

"They was running loose. I drove them back here but they're gone again. They must've had the hell scared out of them."

"All right, hitch my buggy team to Paul's big wagon and let's head for the Broken T. Pull the wagon around in front, and I'll get the bodies wrapped in some quilts. This is awful, awful."

"Yes it is," said Mose, "and it's going to cause just one hell of a stink, Max. People are going to start asking what kind of law enforcement we've got in this county, that something like this could happen."

"You just bring the wagon around and let the law enforcement officer of this county worry about that."

Max meant business, when he was willing to run the hind ends off of his new buggy team and then hook them to Paul's heavy freight wagon. It was the wrong time to rag him. Mose put the buggy team across the tongue of the freight wagon and hooked up the neckyoke all right. He had a hell of a time with the tugs because they had no trace chains, just eyelets in the leather. He had to get the pincers out of Paul's smithy and cut some heavy wire and it seemed to take forever.

Max had tears in his eyes when he came out of the front door of the store and waited. "They won't back worth a damn," Mose called to him. "The wagon is heavier than they're used to backing. We're going to have to tote the bodies further."

"You hold the team. I'll tote them. Get that endgate out first." Max shook his head and then mopped his sweaty face with first one sleeve and then another. "This is awful," he continued. "I think I'll put the straw tick from the bed on the bottom. It's the least we can do."

It would make no difference to Paul and Reva, but Max was right, it was more fitting. Max fixed them a nice bed and carried them out one at a time, rolled up in quilts. Paul Trotter had been a big man, but Max was bigger, and he handled the rigid body easily. He locked in the endgate and climbed up on the seat beside Mose. Mose offered him the lines but Max ignored them.

"Let's go," he said. He put his elbows on his knees and leaned his chin in his hand, not even interested in driving his own new buggy team.

"I ain't going to try it cross-country after dark," Mose said. "Let's stick to the road."

"Yes."

"Hard enough on the team as it is."

"They'll stand it without hurting."

"What'll you do when you get to the Broken T?"

"Have Alec or Edie find someplace where we can leave these poor bodies overnight. Have Alec send a man into town for Grayson Figg. He can round up some men to come out here and give us a hand, come daylight. Who do you think would be worth sending for?"

Grayson Figg was the town doctor, town embalmer, and town postmaster, the latter with the aid of his wife. He also owned a hardware store that was about as high-priced as it could be, and he was tighter than the head on a trap drum. His son-in-law, Bob Kirk, ran the store for him. Mose had disliked Figg for years.

"Well," he said, "you won't find any better men nowhere than the ones Alec works, and you know Alec, he'll drop whatever he's doing to help out when you need him. But Bob Kirk is an all-around good man to have around, too."

"Grayson won't like it."

"Hard lines, is all I say."

"All right, we'll need Bob. A well-matched team there, ain't they?"

"Yes, they come up on the bits real nice. They must be full brothers."

"I thought that myself." Max groaned. "If I was a cursing man, I'd be demanding that God damn the people that done this to death the hardest way He could think of. You had more chance than I did to look around. Did you look around any?"

"As much as I could. I don't claim to be no detective, but I can tell you this much. There was two men riding horses shod all around. They knowed how to tie on and dally, to pull them fences down from the saddle horn. You're going to find that these has been good cowhands *in their time*. Now take note, Max, that I said 'in their time.' Know what I mean by that?"

"That they ain't no more, but I don't see how you're helping me any that way."

"I mean that decent, hard-working cowhands don't do a job of killing this way. They'll shoot up your town for you, or they'll pick a fight with some other outfit and make a regular war of it, or they'll take a notion to wreck a store or a saloon or something in the fall of the year, when it's time to move on."

"Yes, they'll do that, all right, even the best of them. A darned cowboy is completely not responsible or I guess he wouldn't follow the trade."

"Well, thank you for nothing!"

"Present company excepted," Max said soberly. "I mean the drifting rider that just keeps moving around and the only place he gets is old."

"Now you're catching on," said Mose. "Here we've got a couple that used to be good hands but for some reason, they have hit rock bottom. Either they're already wanted by the law for some two-bit stickup, or they've killed somebody somewhere else, or maybe it's just the snakebite remedy. There's more good-looking hands drop in that Alec won't hire because he can tell a bottle-sucker the minute he lays eyes on him. Alec is all right to work for but God, he just has no patience with some things. Abuse an animal, curse in front of his mother or any other lady for that matter, not take a bath—things like that."

Max said nothing; so Mose went on: "I don't claim to be no Sioux when it comes to reading sign, no sir. But I footed it over that place considerable, and I seen where they tied their horses, and I seen how they shot them dogs and the hog, and like that. Now, to me that sign spells it out like a primer, 'I see the cat, Lucy sees the cat, the cat sees us.' Two bottle-suckers down on their luck, spent their summer's pay for a good fall drunk, and maybe the law already on them from somewhere else. What have they got to lose? You know the talk that goes around about the money Paul stashed away!"

"Go on," said Max.

"What you're looking for, Max, is a couple that got fired just before the fall roundup, and why? For going off on a bender, chances are. Couple of boys that could've been pretty good help during the summer, but they couldn't stand prosperity, they had wages to draw and a thirst that had built up all summer, see what I mean?"

"Sometimes," said Max, "you make a surprising amount of sense, Mose."

"Just sometimes? Well, I like that!"

"You talk so durned much most of the time that nobody has a chance to judge you've got a brain."

"Well, I like that, too," said Mose, not at all offended. But when the sheriff did not respond, when he merely sat there on the wagon seat with his elbows on his knees and his feet cocked up on the front endgate, staring forward into the thickening darkness, Mose lost heart. He tried hard to think of something to do to help Max, really help him.

"I reckon I'm out of place," he said, "but if it was me, I'd get on the telegraph and ask every sheriff and police chief from North Platte to Rock Springs to find out if a couple of summer hands that turned out to be bottle-suckers got fired from the same place lately."

"Good idea," the sheriff said, stirring out of his slump and then settling back into it again. "Remind me to write out a wire along them lines to send in when we send for Grayson and Bob."

When "we" send in, the sheriff had said. Mose almost choked, he felt so grateful. He only wished he had the throats of those two killers between his hands this very minute. He'd save the county the cost of a trial and the State of Wyoming the price of a couple of ropes, and that was for damn sure.

"Paul Trotter," he said brokenly, "was the most artful man with tools I ever seen in my life, and so goodhearted, too! He expected you to pay your bills, but he sure gave you your money's worth."

The sheriff seemed to find it hard to speak evenly, too. "Yes," he said, "and you sure don't find that in many places these days. The country is going to heck, Mose. Not many real artisan craftsmen left, nobody cares if they cheat you, and nobody's life is safe."

CHAPTER SEVEN

Sound carried so far after dark fell that the kid could clearly hear the running team on the road. A buggy team, he could tell by the rhythm, and a good one. He came out of his dugout and ran through the darkness toward the sound, gliding along on his moccasins with easy, six-foot strides.

Behind him, he soon heard the gray filly. She was following at a safe distance, but she was following. That made the kid feel good.

He had bought a couple of things at the Trotter place early last summer, but had made himself scarce around there now. He knew the buggy was heading there, and since he was cutting across a hypotenuse, he got there just about the time they came out of the building. He saw the smaller man lean against the wall to twist and light a cigarette while the big one with the full suit of whiskers leaned over and tried to puke his insides out.

The kid had always been scared of Trotter's dogs, but they were dead now, he learned as he listened to the two men talk. So were the Trotters. The kid crept up to within twenty feet of the tied buggy team and heard the whole story.

Nobody had to tell him who had killed those people. Neither did anybody have to tell him who would be blamed for it if he was caught here. Why, folks were going to be so upset over these murders that they would string him up to the nearest tree without giving him a chance to say his prayers!

He had to get out of here. Between the law and those two killers, Ezra and Haze, this part of the world that he had come to regard as his had really been stunk up. Nothing to do now but run.

He ran after watching them bring the bodies out and put them on a straw tick on the wagon bed. The same swift, gliding gait carried him back toward his dugout, his heart pounding wildly, fear making him want to scream like a terrified baby.

And behind him came the gray horse. For the first time, he lost patience with her. "Darn you, Jewel," he sobbed as he ran, "why do you have to butt in all the time? You'll give me away sure. You'll get me hung."

He grounded in his dugout like a fox with the hounds on his trail and lay there shaking all over, as he tried to get his breath back. Now even the dugout was a trap. A dog, any old dog, would track him straight to it. He had nothing much left to eat, not a shell for the old shotgun.

He got his breath back but not his courage. He lay on his stomach and folded his arms under his face, and for the first time in months, he cried. It did not help. It had never helped. For the things that ailed him, nothing helped.

He sat up, his heart pounding again, as he heard *something* padding along the soft dirt of the creek bed just outside his dugout. Oh God, he thought, they've caught me, they'll hang me to one of these oak trees, I'm done for. . . .

And then he realized that it was Jewel he heard—Jewel, come to the very door of his dugout for the first time.

Horses had feelings, too. Jewel did not like the feel of this night any more than he did. Jewel had come to him, and why? Because she needed him and he needed her, that was why.

What a wonderful thing!

And what a coward he had been to think of running! Jewel hadn't run, except to him. Jewel's faith in him—well, it was just wonderful, that was all. He had to live up to it some way. How?

There was nothing harder to face than the truth, but Jewel's faith nerved him to do it. He had to find where Haze and Ezra had gone and keep track of them until he could tell a policeman somewhere. He was going to be in a peck of trouble when he did that. He would lose everything, just everything that made life worth living to him, the minute he showed his face to a policeman, but he just plain had to do it.

Or, rather, he and Jewel had to do it together. Haze and Ezra were mounted, and Jewel had to carry him, too. She wasn't going to like it a bit, not at first, but she just plain had to do it. And the time to start was now, while it was still dark and she was tired and had a full stomach and was lonesome for him. By daylight, maybe Jewel would be content to carry him.

He picked up the coiled rope that had been left for him on the rock, and came out of the dugout. "Steady, Jewel," he said, but seeing him down on all fours spooked her. She snorted and ran.

He clambered up the creek bank and stood under the shelter of the oaks. There was no moon, but there were jillions of stars, more stars here in Wyoming, he guessed, than anywhere else in the world. They had a bigger sky in Wyoming than anywhere else, probably.

He walked out of the trees, carrying the coiled rope and watching Jewel. He came to a stop and just stood there, as close to motionless as he could be. Jewel knew he was there but she tried to pretend she did not. She tried to pretend she was hungry, ripping up grass and then not chewing it, tossing it aside and ripping up some more.

Foolish old curious nosy Jewel finally could not stand it any more. Here she came, tail up, picking her feet up in that fancy way she had when she wanted to show off. The kid just stood there. She came to within fifty feet of him and whirled suddenly as though a mountain lion were about to leap on her.

The kid just stood there. She turned again and on she came, forgetting to prance, forgetting to heist her tail and be playful. The kid just stood there. Five minutes later, she came up for him to lean against her and scratch her between the ears and under the jaw. The kid just stood there.

Jewel looked around at him through the dark as though to ask, "Why aren't you leaning against me? Why aren't you scratching me? What's wrong?" He knew her well enough by now to know that she was a flirt, she took some handling.

"Listen," he said, "you're not going to like this, Jewel darling, but we've got to go on to something new. And I've got to have you over closer to those trees to do it. So you come on."

He walked to the trees and passed his rope around the nearest one. Jewel followed only so far. He came back to her slowly, carrying both ends of the rope. They looked at each other. He thought that Jewel was a little suspicious, but she was always getting suspicious on him. That did not worry him.

In a minute she came up to be leaned against, and he leaned against her. When he reached over her neck to scratch under her jaw, he passed the rope around her neck. She did not notice it. He threw a quick bowline in the rope and then, with the bight of it, took a quick half-hitch around her nose. He hated to do it to her, but at the same time it was quite a thrill, too.

He had a hackamore on her now and the rope snubbed around a tree. She could kick and snort and have a fit if she liked, but a bowline wouldn't choke up like a slipknot and he could hold her snubbed up forever if he had to.

"But I hope it won't have to be that way, Jewel darling," he said. "We've got to learn together. We've got—"

Wups! She felt the rope, flinched back, and felt it take hold of her entire head. The head had never been imprisoned before. It was fastened to her body, which meant that her body was now imprisoned, too. All of her was neatly held by that strange rope around her head. What had always been wild and free was now a prisoner, all of her.

The kid began to cry as she whirled and kicked and bucked, eyes rolling wildly in the dark as she fought to get back her lost freedom. "I sure hate this, Jewel," he said, between sobs, "but what else can I do? Please, Jewel. Please be nice!"

By talking and talking and talking, by paying out a little rope and then snubbing up again when she went ramping and romping closer to the tree, he finally showed her that she wasn't going to get away no matter what. Well, there she stood, shivering in the dark, eyes still rolling so he could see the whites shine, breathing hard and fluttering her nostrils in a snort every now and then.

The kid let her stand. He stood still, too, and kept talking. He had quit crying, thrilled with having been right about winning this dispute with her. She had done exactly what he had expected her to do, and by golly he was going to ride her, too! He knew that in his heart as he had known the other in his heart.

He kept talking, talking, talking, and his talk was about the only familiar thing left in the world to the trapped horse. Maybe she blamed him for trapping her, maybe she didn't. Maybe she thought they were both trapped, and maybe she was right if she thought that. The thing was, she had stopped fighting. The thing was, she still needed him.

It was as though she said, "Hey, kid, I'm not sure about you now. I don't know what you've done to me, kid, and you surely can understand that! And if you don't, and you take any chances with me, I'm going to feel perfectly free to kick your brains out of you. But look here, kid, something is surely wrong, and you have always treated me right up to now. What I want to know is—are we in this together, or aren't we?"

Something like that. He went up to her an inch at a time, keeping the rope taut. She rolled her eyes at him menacingly. She cocked a hind foot and dared him. Before she could kick, he stepped in close and leaned against her. She couldn't kick with him that close.

"Stop trembling, Jewel," he said. "You're just being foolish. You remind me more of a kitten than a horse, for gosh sake! Now listen here, Jewel, in a few minutes I'm going to get up astraddle and ride you. You think you're not going to like it, but look at the fix you're in and tell me what good is it going to do to make a lot of fuss?"

Time passed. She stopped trembling. He let the rope go a little slack, to rest her neck, and she seemed to appreciate that. He was on the right side of her, and he had to get on the left to mount her. He passed behind her, keeping the rope taut and letting it pass over her, and she did not flinch.

But now he had it to do all over again from the left side. Just lean there. Talk, talk, talk. Give her a pat now and then, a scratch. Put a little more weight on her. Squat and stand up, squat and stand up until she got used to that.

And finally squat and give a little jump. He was on her. Throw a leg across, keeping the rope taut. She just stood there. He just sat there.

Jewel took a step forward with the kid on her back. He took in the slack. He could feel her relax under him and he knew that suddenly she was used to it, suddenly she had decided that this was something she just had to put up with. He tried changing his seat, shifting around, making free with legs and heels against her.

She just stood here. The kid felt like crying again, or whooping, he was not sure which. When he slid off, Jewel did not seem to care one way or the other. When he got back on, she just stood there. He did that again and again —off, on, off, on, off, on—until she was bored with it.

He slid off and went to her head. "Now, Jewel," he said, "we're going to make me a pair of reins, and you're going to learn to neck-rein. I wish I had me a martingale because a martingale shortens this part of it quite a bit. But Jewel honey, even if you buck me off a dozen times, you're still going to learn to carry me. Oh, you're the most beautiful horse that ever lived in the world!"

CHAPTER EIGHT

Ma was fooling around with the piano when Alec got home. He could hear the music—or noise, whichever it was—all the way to the corral. Tango Tangerus came out to take his horse. He whistled when he saw Little Si.

"Wondered how you'd get home," he said. "Your horse come in a minute ago. Didn't tell your mother lest it upset her. Is this our horse now? He sure is a little runt up close, ain't he?"

"I just borrowed him," Alec growled, "and he's the best cutting horse I ever saw, and I'd like to own him someday."

He let Tango take care of Little Si and went on into the house. You could tell how Ma was suffering by the agony in the piano chords. The piano had belonged to a rich Iowa family that went broke, and Ma had made Reed Pitman haul it all the way to Wyoming although it took a heavy-duty wagon and two extra teams.

"This is how you acquire the good things of life," Alec's daddy had said more than once. "You get a wife that wants them. Well, I came out of it with a wagon I wouldn't've had otherwise."

It was what they called a concert grand, German made, about the size of a mahogany hay barn with keys of real African ivory and African ebony. Alec had had a separate room built on the house for it, with a chimney and a stove of its own. Ma had fits when she tried to learn to play, using Professor Friedrich Schnabel's *Eclectic Self-Teacher for the Pianoforte,* which had cost Reed Pitman another three dollars.

She was flailing away at some old church hymn tonight, "A Mighty Fortress Is Our God," which nobody on earth could sing anyway, Alec thought. He opened the door to the music room because she demanded that he pay his respects to her every time he came home from anywhere. He stood watching her a moment, his resentment all slipping away from him.

How beautiful she was! How young-looking with all that gray hair over that creamy, unlined face! Slim as a girl, quick-moving and graceful, and with the profile of a Spanish queen.

She fought a pair of chords to a draw, gave up, and buried her face in her arms over the keys. "Ah-h-h," she wept, the same sound the average woman would make hearing her only son condemned to hang.

"I thought you just about had it there," Alec said. "It's the damn song's fault. Don't feel bad—that's just an ugly song, that's all."

She took her hands away from her tear-wet face. It was the face of a passionate little girl of seven who knew that life was just about over for her and not a damn thing accomplished.

"It's me, not the music," she said, flinging her hands out. "I've almost had it for a year. I know it in my mind and in my heart, but I'm too old to know it in my hands. I'm too old for everything. I don't know why I don't just lie down and die."

He leaned in the doorway. "Of all the ignorant things to say! You look younger than me, your own son."

"What have you been up to? You never bother to be nice unless you've got a guilty conscience."

"It ain't my conscience makes me look this way. I'm starved, is all. I want my supper."

"Oh, really!" she said, standing up. "I thought you'd have had supper with your widow-woman. All the comforts of home, you know. I wonder that you can look your mother in the eye after where you've spent the afternoon."

In a minute they were quarreling, and again and again he had vowed never to let her tease him into it. He remembered that before he went so far as to swear, and turned his back on her and headed for the kitchen. But she followed him all the way.

"How can you, Alec? The woman just doesn't care what talk goes on about her."

"Exactly what talk, Ma? About me? I haven't seen her in a month and a half."

"Her and that nasty, thieving Dave Conn."

"I'll second that motion, about Dave."

In the kitchen, he peeled off his coat to hang it on his private hook in the corner. Ma continued to scold.

"What he's doing to that poor, deluded James is a crime. The man should be horsewhipped. If your father were alive, he would be. James is an innocent baby, so helpless. That's what decency does, it weakens you in the face of the evil in men like Dave Conn. I feel *so* sorry for poor James, but what can I do?"

He lifted the lid from a pot on the stove and saw beef stew and some dumplings that had gone soggy and looked extra delicious. A dumpling wasn't a dumpling until it had soaked up some gravy. There were fried potatoes in the skillet, and in the warming closet half a mincemeat pie. There was venison in that mincemeat, and Ma made the best mincemeat and the best piecrust he had ever eaten.

"James?" he said. "James who?" It dawned on him what she meant, and it was such a shocker that he said one of the forbidden words. "You mean old Buck Buchert for Christ's sake? He ain't innocent, he's just dumb."

"Feed yourself!" she screamed at him. "I get so *damned* tired of setting two tables just so you can chase after that Butterworth woman. Why can't she feed you there? You don't see James hanging around there like a street dog. How you can come back here and face me, your own mother, after you've been with her, well it's just the last straw."

She flounced out, and by God she was beautiful, and no two ways about it. And in love with old Buck Buchert! Stuck on him like a schoolgirl. The shock was something he'd have to get used to.

He got a plate out, but then Ma's kitchen helper, Duke Palmer, came in and snarled at him, "Set down and I'll feed you. I don't know why you can't git home in time to eat when the others do."

He sat down. Duke was an average old loafer, but Ma had whipped him into shape so he stayed clean and did a good job, and he had a right to think of himself as a privileged character. All the cooking was done in this kitchen, but the crew's dining room had been built on the rear. Usually Alec ate with the men, but he sat at the round table in the kitchen corner tonight.

"Duke," he said, "would you call Buck Buchert innocent?"

"Of work, yes," said Duke. "Don't let your ma know I said that, though. You know what she said the other day?

She said he was prematurely aged because of the hard life he'd had to live, and I said yes, Buck rocked a rocking chair harder than anybody I ever knowed. It was just a joke, you see, but say! Your ma like to brained me with a stove lid."

"Think she's in love with him, Duke?"

"Of course she is."

"Ain't she pretty old for that?"

"You young fellas give me a pain in the hind end. I suppose you think I'm too old for it, too."

Alec looked him over carefully. "I never gave it a thought before, Duke," he said, "but no, I think you'll be too old for it when you're about ninety-two."

He sent Duke away happy, after he had washed the dishes and poured the dishwater into the slop pail for the hogs. Duke would preen on that for a year now. Alec got his pipe off the shelf and loaded it with shag, and sat down with something to ponder for his nightly smoke this time.

Buck Buchert for a stepdaddy! Ma or somebody would have to make the first move. Buck couldn't get off his shoulder blades long enough to woo a woman, even if Dave Conn would let him.

It was worth thinking about. They could fix up Buck's house and live there, and he felt good all over at the thought of having this place to himself, so he could bring Esther Butterworth here.

Say! Make one cattle ranch of the Broken T, Buck's Bar X, and Esther's Four Plus. Between graze, hay land and what you could crop on Esther's place, you'd have a property that could pay as well as any in Wyoming.

Buck wouldn't mind being bossed around by Ma. It was what he needed. Dave Conn alone stood in the way there, just as he stood in the way with Esther. Alec's pipe went out and he forgot to light it again, as he pondered his plans and his problems. It was always smart to think as many things out ahead of time as possible, and the way it was beginning to look to Alec, Dave Conn had become something more than a pest. He was suddenly downright surplus.

He could hear old loudmouthed Mose jawing away, and went out in his sock feet to see the wagon bring in Paul and Reva Trotter's bodies. Mose was just about hysterical. Sheriff Max Maddox seemed dazed, and it was hard for Alec not to start raking him over the coals. You had to give a man a chance to get moving, and Alec knew he already had the reputation of being too much of a manager.

Ma heard them, too, and saw the lanterns as the crew turned out and put Max's new buggy team away. She did not cry. She was not a crying woman, not even when she gave birth to Alec at the age of not quite seventeen. She was just crushed, that was all, when Max turned down her offer to take care of Reva's body.

"I've done it before," she said. "My God, if you think I haven't prepared a body for burial! I owe her that much."

Max shook his head. "It's a doctor's job, Edie. You wouldn't like the sight of her."

Alec put his arm around his mother. "Why don't you get a bait of grub ready for the boys to take with them in the morning? My hunch is that Max will want to hit the trail before daylight." He looked at the sheriff. "We'll all ride with you, Max."

Max nodded and stroked his beard. "Like to set down

and talk things over with you first, Alec. If I could have a cup of coffee, maybe?"

It was a question, and Ma answered it by stuffing the kitchen firebox full of pine knots and putting on the pot. They could not get rid of her until she had put a pan of cornbread in the oven and put the skillet on with some bacon in it. She had Alec so nervous he was ready to explode before she finally said, "There, you can fry the bacon and set the coffee back when it boils. No need to wake Duke. I'll need him in the morning."

Duke could sleep through a cyclone. Alec tended the bacon and kept an eye on the cornbread and coffee, waiting for Max to make up his mind to speak. It began to look like he never would. Alec put the grub out on the table, bacon, cornbread, and honey and wild plum butter both. The sheriff fell to it like a starving wolf, but Alec could see him struggling to make up his mind to say what he had to say.

At last Alex had to pry it out of him. "Where'd you get that new team? Very handsome pair, and Mose just purely loves them."

Max squirmed. "I wish I'd never seen them," he groaned. "If Mose can track and read sign, and—oh heck, Alec, I don't need him to read it for me. There was two of them in on that murder."

"And they got something to do with your new team?" Alec prompted him.

He thought Max was going to burst into tears. It came out haltingly, but it came out. Max had never had any ambitions to own a fine buggy team and buggy, not on his salary. But he got to talking to this fellow who knew of a team and buggy for sale by an estate. The old woman who was inheriting just wanted to get rid of them and get her hands on the cash. All this fellow that had told Max about it wanted was fifty dollars for telling him about the deal. If it wasn't worth it when he saw the team and buggy, he didn't owe him anything.

Well, the next day they were in the town wagon lot, and team, harness and buggy could be bought for two hundred dollars. Add fifty to that for the inside information and you still had a pair and buggy that you could turn over for four hundred dollars any day you wanted to. Just let it be known you could be talked into a sale and they'd stomp all over you to bid on it.

There weren't that many people able to pay four hundred dollars for a fancy team and buggy, or even three hundred or two hundred. "Where the hell would you get two hundred and fifty dollars, Max?" Alec asked.

"I had the fifty," Max moaned, "and I went to the bank for the two hundred."

Alec was hard put not to shake his head in despair. Max was not the worst man ever to be elected sheriff, but he certainly was not the brightest, either. And he had the office and a murder to deal with, and this was no time to unman him. Bullying, Esther Butterworth would call it.

"Damn it, man," Alec said, "if you needed that little dab of money you should've come to me. But I'm about to make you a little bet that that team and buggy was in charge of a pair of sonsabitches riding horses shod all around. Men you never seen before and ain't seen since."

"Well," Max whimpered, "there was a lawyer by the name of Fitz came in by train from Cheyenne with the bill of sale, and he got the money. But I *did* see these two that had delivered the team and buggy. I seen Fitz pay them ten dollars apiece."

"Something here I don't get," Alec said. "They had

their own horses but they drove this team here, is that it? All the way from Cheyenne?"

Max said, from the depths of misery, "Fitz said the outfit was first sold to a fella by the name of Chet Blankenship—"

"I know Chet. Where the hell would he find the money for an outfit like that?"

"That was the trouble, he couldn't. So they come on here, another forty-odd miles, and wired Fitz. And he told me he was so dang fed up with this old woman and that team and buggy, he told them to sell for two hundred if they could get cash and he'd take the first train west. A couple of cars went on the ground just this side of Laramie, so they was late getting into town."

Max tugged at his beard and rolled his eyes. *If* the train had not been late, *if* he had not had time to try the team out, *if* Fitz had got there to sell them himself—none of this would have happened.

"I know," Alec said. "Well, all we can do is go after them. I don't suppose you got a very good look at them. You was too busy looking at the team."

"That's about the size of it."

"Nobody will hear about it from me, Max."

"You're a good man, Alec, and a good friend. I don't suppose you'd like to take that team and buggy off my hands for what I've got in them?"

"Let me think about it. I still don't see why you didn't come to me in the first place for the money. I ain't exactly a greenhorn in a horse deal, and if a man in your position is going to borrow money, it's better not to go through a damn bank."

"I know," said Max, "but I knowed there was some hard feelings on your part, and in fact when I mentioned

I might raise the money from you, he said hell no, if you was in the deal, there wasn't going to be no deal."

"Who said that?"

"The fella that first told me about the team and buggy," said Max. "Dave Conn."

Alec was not really surprised. He had felt from the first that Dave wasn't to be trusted anywhere, with anything. Dave had worked his tail off for better than two years now, mismanaging the Bar X, hoping to be a big cattleman and a respectable man in the community someday. He surely knew by now that he wasn't going to make it that way. He wasn't making wages.

Wherefore he was cashing in as fast as he could, every way he could. Witness the fifty he had taken from Alec for the gray filly today, as well as the fifty from Max. He could have quite a bit of traveling money stored up, selling Buck's belongings off a little at a time. What held him back from traveling, then? Alec knew the answer to that, too.

Esther Butterworth.

He held his temper, kept cool, let his mind race, and grabbed an idea when he needed it. "It's spilled milk, Max," he said. "You don't think Dave was in on these killings, surely."

"No, no. My stars, Dave wouldn't do a thing like that!"

Alec was not so sure, but he kept his thoughts on that subject to himself. "I've got something I've just got to do, first thing in the morning," he said, "but Mose can get as much out of my boys as I can, and he's got a good head on him. If my crew can't track these bastards down and either bring them in or kill them, nobody can. You go out there to the bunkhouse now, and turn in until Duke calls you for breakfast."

He reached across the table and laid his hand on the sheriff's arm. "Everything will look better in the morning. When you see somebody you've knowed and liked that's been murdered, it kind of knocks you off your pegs, don't it? Well, in the morning you'll be as mad as ever, but fighting mad, not scared mad. Come on, I'll take you down there myself."

"You're a good friend," Max said.

Mose was jawing away, telling the story for the umpteenth time and keeping the crew awake when they needed their rest for tomorrow. Alec called him outside and told him how to help Max tomorrow, how to back him up without stepping on his official corns, how to keep Max's nose to the trail.

"You've got to make him think he thought of things," he said. "The responsibility will be yours but you'll never get any credit for it. I'm depending on you to see that the Broken T gives a good account of itself."

Mose was trembling all over with eagerness to live up to the charge Alec had given him. "Do the very best I can, Alec," he said. "Paul and Reva was my friends, too."

"Yes," said Alec. "Now go back in there and shut up your big mouth and let everybody get some sleep."

CHAPTER NINE

Draining that pus pocket had done the trick for Haze. His jaw was still sore, but by evening he could chew some of the grub they had brought from the Trotter place, using the teeth he had left on the other side. He still suffered for a drink, and so did Ezra, but there was nothing they could do about that yet.

They pushed their horses hard, in their imaginations hearing a posse thundering up behind them every foot of the way. Haze was lost here, but Ezra had been all over this country. He knew a place up near the Powder River where they could rest up, if their damned old horses could stand the pace that far. Then on to Crazy Woman Creek, where Ezra had more friends. Closer friends, too.

"Then what?" Haze asked.

"This fella, he knows of a country bank in Idaho that four men can take easy," said Ezra.

"Him and us only make three."

"Jesus Christ, I can add! He's got one man. He's got the horses, too."

"How much you reckon is in that bank?"

"He says he heard the banker say that he never carries less than five or six thousand in cash. Now, Morgan wants the first thousand for himself, because it's his deal. The rest we split four ways."

"Morgan is your friend's name?"

"You ask the most ignorant questions, Haze. Now who the hell do you think he is?"

They had quarreled like this ever since fate had thrown them together in the Cheyenne jail. They were not congenial companions because neither was capable of congeniality with any other human being. They were both loners, but not lone wolves. They had the voracity of hungry wolves, but not their courage.

Ezra thought he had more courage than Haze, but the fact that he could bully Haze, that Haze let himself be bullied, did not prove heart or the absence of heart, or even a difference in degree of heart. Ezra snarled out of habit. So did Haze, when he had a mouth fit for it. His was getting better, but he felt no gratitude toward Ezra for that crude, healing surgery. When he thought of that knife, he hated Ezra as he had never hated anyone in the world.

"The one thing that worries me," Haze said.

"What?" said Ezra.

"This Morgan, if his plan ain't no better than the one you had for cleaning out that old son of a bitch of a blacksmith, we'll be no better off a month from today than we are today. Worse, maybe."

Ezra, riding in the lead, turned his tired horse in a fury and drove in his spurs. He forced his horse into Haze's and tried to knock it backward, but Haze rammed in the spurs, too. The horses took the abuse the two men could not vent on each other.

"I ought to kill you for that," said Ezra.

"Try it," said Haze. He knew that he was a far better shot with a .45 than Ezra. Being this close, no more than four feet apart, being a good shot didn't amount to a hill of beans. But it still gave him the Indian sign on Ezra, and he knew it.

"No use of us falling out, Haze," Ezra said. "We're in this together."

"In what together?" said Haze. "I just done what you said to do, that's all."

"You bent that woman's finger back and broke it yourself."

"You told me to." When Ezra merely made a gurgling sound of despair and rage, Haze went on, "We're in a hell of a fix and we might as well face it. And I'll tell you something else, I want to know a hell of a lot more about your friend, Morgan's, plan before I go into it than I did about this deal. This is a hanging matter, a *hanging* matter, and what did we get out of it? Less than twenty dollars."

"That stubborn old son of a bitch—"

"You're the one that killed her, Ezra. That was when he got stubborn. What did he have to lose after she died? And you can't say I didn't try to tell you, because I did."

Ezra's whole lower jaw quivered. "It's all right with me if we part right now. If you don't want to go in with Morgan and me, I'll find somebody with some guts."

"I didn't say I wouldn't, I just said I wanted to know what kind of a plan he had before I go into it. That's all I said, and after the way you let us both in for a hanging, that's the way I feel."

"I got a good notion to split from you right now," Ezra said, his whole lower jaw quivering again in his rage. "You go your way and I'll go mine. Hell, you're lost! You don't even know where you are, you Goddamn fool. I have to take care of you like a baby. I had to cure your tooth and now I got to lead you like a tenderfoot and then cut you in on a plan to stick up a bank. I will like hell! You go your way and I go mine."

Haze slowly drew his gun. "You just try that. You're going to lead the way and never get out of this forty-five's range because you ain't leaving me out in no strange country like this. So lead on."

Ezra led on. For a while they rode in silence, but neither man could stand silence and his own thoughts. What they had done yesterday filled their thoughts, and while neither suffered from pangs of conscience, both were able to realize that they were indeed in bad, bad trouble. The truth was, they *had* to stick together. Neither trusted the other out of his sight.

Shortly they began talking again:

"I don't know about your horse," Ezra said, "but this skate is about played out."

"We ain't went very far," said Haze, "but this faithless bastard sure ain't going much farther for me."

Ezra stood up in the saddle to study what he could see of the sun. They were in rough graze now, foothills covered with vividly tinted softwood trees. Ezra had counted on putting a lot more miles behind them than this, but there was no use killing their horses and finding themselves afoot tomorrow.

"We better make camp, Haze. Catch a little sleep and rest the horses, and then see."

"Where are we, anyhow?"

Ezra grinned, and to Haze it was like a skull's grin. "Don't you wish you knowed!"

Again Haze drew his gun. "I want to know where the hell we are!"

"What good would it do to tell you? I think we're still in Albany County. On the other hand, we can't be far from Converse County. Now do you know any more than you did before?"

Haze rubbed his sore jaw. The swelling had gone down and now the wound from where the knife had gone in had started to itch and ache at the same time. But although this was a good sign, since itching usually meant healing, he went suddenly still all over with terror.

"Listen!" he hissed.

"What?"

"Cowbell, sounded like."

They listened. The sound came again, distantly. Ezra drew down his skull's mouth at both ends to keep his jaw from trembling again.

"No nesters around here that I know of," he said. "Somebody's milk cow run off and went wild, is all it could be. Or say, that could be the bell on the lead mule of a pack train."

"Either way, I don't like it. Ezra." Haze stared at his partner, lost his head, and shouted at the top of his voice, "Ezra! What the hell is the matter with you, Ezra?"

Ezra had first hoisted his left arm with a grimace of pain. He opened his mouth and a strange sound came out of it. He opened it still wider, as though gasping for air. The arm dropped. So did the reins he held in his other hand.

Ezra went limp. His head tilted forward, his whole body tilted forward, and he toppled out of the saddle and fell in a heap on his head and did not move. His weary horse merely stepped aside and let him fall.

Haze dismounted and knelt beside the limp form and took it by the shoulders. "Ezra, are you all right? What's the matter with you? Why the hell don't you answer me?" he implored his partner.

Ezra's eyes were half open, half shut. His mouth gaped open, and he was already turning gray in the skin. Haze let him drop and put his ear against Ezra's chest. Hearing nothing, he fumbled at his wrist—at his other wrist—at the artery he used to see throbbing at the base of Ezra's throat when he got good and mad.

Nothing. Heart failure! The double-crossing son of a bitch had dropped dead on him out here in the middle of nowhere.

CHAPTER TEN

Three hours of sleep were all that Alec allowed himself. Usually Duke got breakfast, but Edie had had a bad night, and when Alec came down to the kitchen she was starting to cook and giving Duke hell.

"Why didn't you sleep in?" Alec asked her. "Duke could've fed us."

"How could a body sleep? Those two poor old people out there in a wagon box haunt me," she said.

"I know how you feel," he said, and he did. He put his arm around her to prove it, and she forgot how mad she was at him over the Widow Butterworth and leaned against him to cry against his chest.

"They deserved better of this country. Paul helped make it a decent place to live. When your father and I—"

She began boohooing and could not go on. Just when you got so mad at Ma you were ready to belt her over the head with a stick of stovewood, here she came like the U.S. Cavalry. Ma's trouble, it suddenly seemed to him, was that he had become a grownup before she had. What she needed was someone to take care of—old Buck Buchert, for instance.

He had time for a word or two with Mose Henry before Duke called the others to breakfast. Mose was quieter than Alec had ever seen him. There was a good chance that responsibility today would keep his mouth shut so all his brains wouldn't run out. Alec warned him to keep an eye out for two things—himself and the kid who had walked down the gray horse.

"You figger to run that little varmint down today? Why?" Mose asked.

"I'll tell you that," said Alec, "after I've catched him—if I catch him."

Just for contrariness, he rode Buck Buchert's Little Si horse, which looked like it could go all day and not tire. What was really a bloodcurdling thought was that if Dave Conn was cashing in everything he could, what if he dealt Little Si off to somebody coming through who did not ask questions? I'd hate to lose this horse, Alec thought, as though Little Si were already his. . . .

It was just coming daylight when he dismounted and led the little stud up the slope to the grove where Mose had first shown him the kid. It was the kind of morning that Alec Pitman loved, with a heavier frost than you usually got at this time of year making the ground sparkle, and not three cents' worth of clouds in the sky. But Paul and Reva Trotter would not enjoy this morning. They would never enjoy another, and for this he could thank Dave Conn.

Proving Dave's responsibility to the satisfaction of the law might be impossible. Probably would be. But even a man as rotten to the heart as Dave would know that he had worn out his welcome here. All Max Maddox had to do was talk about that buggy and buggy team, and Dave was through. And Max had talked to Alec.

He forgot all about the mess that had spoiled things for everybody when he got to the shelter of the little grove. He knew instantly that he was beholding a wonderful thing down there near Buford Creek. To the end of his life he would remember this, and take comfort in it and the way it proved that the whole human race was not entirely worthless. It still paid to aspire, to take risks, to dedicate yourself to one noble job no matter how people laughed at it.

That kid was riding that gray filly!

Had been riding her most of the night, the way both of them were sagging. Had made himself a hackamore and a pair of lines out of Mose Henry's old rope, and was neck-reining her, sitting with a cavalryman's hard butt even though he had no saddle at all. He had been taught to ride on an English or a McClellan saddle, that was a cinch.

Walk. Trot. Canter a little. Stop. Turn. Back up, although she did not do this very well and probably would not without a bit in her mouth. Turn the other way. Trot, with the kid's hand on his hip and his elbow out like a cavalry instructor's teaching close-order horse drill.

The kid pulled her in and slid down and went to her head. He threw his arms around her head and pressed his face into her poll, where her scruffy mane began between her ears. The filly nuzzled him a little but mostly just stood there, grateful to rest.

How that boy did love that worthless horse! Alec wished he could paint a picture of that, or make a statue of it.

The kid turned her free and slumped down into the frosty grass and locked his arms around his knees. The filly wandered down toward the creek as if to drink. The kid called something after her. It was too far for Alec to hear the words, but he could see the horse respond by looking back. She did not stop, but she made sure he was there.

Alec climbed up on Little Si as soon as the filly had vanished down in the creek bed. He gave the little stud a prod with his heels, and Si stretched himself. By the time the weary kid heard, it was too late to run for his hidey in the creek bed.

Besides, he was too tired to make up his mind that fast. Besides, he was staring at Little Si as though he had never seen a horse in his life. When he realized that Alec could get between him and creek if he felt like it, he was too proud to make a run for it. He just stood there.

Seeing him do that, Alec did not try to get between him and the creek. He rode straight down and hauled Little Si in with a flourish, holding his right hand up in a peace sign, palm toward the kid.

"Howdy, son," he said.

"I'm not your son," said the kid.

"No, but I'd be proud if you was. You walked that filly down, didn't you? I'd've bet you a thousand dollars to a ten-spot that it couldn't be done. I know I couldn't. That's just about the greatest thing I ever seen in my whole life."

The kid's face lighted up briefly, but he held his tongue.

"Like my horse?" said Alec. "He ain't really mine, but I'm sure going to make a try to deal for him."

"He's beautiful," said the kid, "but not as beautiful as my horse." He said the "my" part defiantly, for which Alec admired him.

"What I wanted to tell you, son," said Alec, "is that that gray really is your horse. I saw you with her yesterday, and I went and bought her for you from the owner."

"Honest?"

"Honest. You're about the best horseman I've ever saw, probably the best in the world, and anybody who could do what you done deserves the horse. What do you call her?"

"I call her Jewel."

"That's fine, that's a pretty name. What's yours?"

"I'm not going to tell you that."

"You don't have to if you don't want to, but I've got to call you something. I want you to go to work for me. I've got one little job I want you to do first, and then I've got a bunch of colts I want you to break for me. How old are you?"

"I won't tell you that, either."

"That's all right with me, but I'll tell you what, I pay a top hand forty a month during the haying season and roundup. You're as tall as I am, almost, but I doubt you're fifteen yet. But I'll go as high as fifty a month, beginning right this morning, if you'll go to work for me and break my colts."

The kid said nothing. He was plainly not impressed by fifty dollars a month, either. Alec thought he had him trotting, though, with the promise of a job breaking colts.

"Cat got your tongue?"

"You scared my horse off!"

"Yes, I did, but I bought her for you and I can get her back for you. I can do a lot of things for you, and I'd be glad to, and I'll tell you why. I like a man that knows how to handle a horse. That's the main thing. You're well bespoke, too, you've probably got more education than I have already, and you come from a good family. I can tell that, see, just what little we've talked. Now, I don't know why you run off from home, or where home is, or who your family is, and right now I plain don't care."

He kept talking; Esther would have called it bullying, and she would have been right. The kid did not know he was being bullied. He thought—as Alec meant him to think—that here was a real tough old man being real nice to him. He thought this tough old man was talking to him man to man, always a flattering proposition to a growing boy.

In a way, he was. In another way, he was walking the kid down same as the kid had walked the gray horse down. Somehow, even as he kept on talking, Alec remembered a time when he had gone into the bank not long after his daddy had died. He wasn't even shaving more than once a month then, but he had sat down at the president's desk and put his old hat on the corner and dragged a bunch of messy papers out of his pocket.

Angus Dunbar, who had founded the bank, was alive then. What Angus ran he ran with no advice and very little help. "A bank exists to serve the community," he often said, "but I decide how it serves. When you come in for a loan, come to the point because I've got no patience with time-wasters. I'll tell you in short order if we can accommodate you, and all the palaver in the world won't change my mind."

Alec had known that, and yet he said, "Ma and me need four thousand dollars. Or I do. Ma don't know what she needs, but she ain't running the Broken T, I am. I'm already up to my ass in debt—I don't need to tell you that, Angus, but here's what we're going to do."

The old devil had flinched a little to hear a fresh kid call him "Angus," but he listened, and he studied the papers as Alec shoved them over to him. So much for barbwire to fence off the whole north slope for hay meadows. So much for two half-blood Galloway bulls. So much to add two rooms to the house so Alec would have a bedroom of his own. So much for a haystacker, so much for six sets of new harness, so much for this and that and the other.

"This comes to six thousand," said Angus.

"Yes. I'm going to sell off a lot of worthless cow stock. Cull the bejesus out of them while prices are right. That was the next thing my daddy was going to do. Don't do no good to bring in new bulls and breed them to scrub cows. Oh, sure, it helps. You improve the herd, but not fast enough."

"So this is what we're going to do."

"Yes."

"You're an impudent little bastard, kid. Alec is a Scots name. You must have some Scots blood in you."

"Grandma Pitman's maiden name was McDonald. I was named for her father, Alec McDonald."

"See, I sensed that!" Mr. Dunbar said with a pleased smile.

"To tell you the truth, Ma don't talk much about her father. He had a ladies' clothing store, and he couldn't leave them alone. Or so my daddy said. The ladies, I mean. He got caught in bed once too often with somebody's wife, and Daddy said the old hellion was close to seventy when he was shot."

"Shot to death?"

"Yes. So Ma don't talk much about him, but I think she's still pretty proud of him."

Angus Dunbar said she had a right to be, and approved the loan immediately. He never knew that Alec barely made it to the hitch rail back of the bank before his knees caved in on him. After old Angus had his stroke and had to retire, Alec used to drop in and see him. The whole left side of his face sagged, and he gobbled when he tried to talk, but he did not seem to be ashamed to have Alec see him that way. He always had his wife trot out a bottle and pour two big slugs of it.

"To Grandpa McDonald," he'd say when he hoisted his.

"He carried the flag," Alec would say.

"Once too often," Angus would say.

Yes, sir, Alec knew how much it could mean to a kid to have a grown man, an important man, take him seriously enough to talk to him man-to-man. He got down off Little Si to make a cigarette, and, playing a hunch, let the reins drop. The kid plainly had never had anything to do with a cutting horse, never knew that a working cow horse would "stand tied" to the ground that way. He jumped to catch the reins before Little Si got away.

"Oh, he'll stand there until he starves to death. That's the way he's trained," Alec said. "That's how I want all of my colts trained. A horse you can't trust to stay where he belongs is worthless."

"I never knew that."

"Why don't you try him out, son? Your legs is almost as long as mine. Ever ride a stock saddle like that?"

"No."

"Thought not. You learned on a McClellan, I'll bet, and took lessons."

"English. Thanks."

The kid was not a word-waster. He got up on Little Si's back and walked him a few steps, was all.

"Stirrups too long, sir."

"No, you don't set that saddle like you do an English saddle. Straighten your legs out so you can ride on your butt or your feet, either one, because that's a working saddle on a working horse. Go ahead, put him into a run! I'll bet you never rode a smoother ride in your life."

The kid's face just shone when he came back with Little Si, and he had already adjusted to the saddle. He dismounted and, without a word, dropped the reins over the horse's head. He was plain delighted to see Little Si slouch there like he was tied.

"Ever use a rope, son?"

"No."

"That's something you'll have to learn, but there's no hurry about it. I'll go catch your gray for you, and let's head for home. What am I going to call you—Montmorency?"

"Why Montmorency?"

Alec grinned. "Well, you won't tell me your real name, and you're an educated youngster that had riding lessons on an English saddle, and all that spells something pretty fancy to me. Montmorency is about the fanciest name I can think of."

"No, my name's not that," the kid said, his face getting that closed look.

"Monte? Would you answer to that? I've got to call you something."

"All right," the kid said, with an unwilling smile, "Monte, I like that."

Alec finished his cigarette and ground it out under his heel, lecturing the kid on grass fires. He mounted Little Si and went after the gray, which was far beyond the creek. Alec was pretty pleased with himself. The kid never had said yes or no, but he had let Alec hire him and name him. Sometimes you had to sneak up on people that way, like getting a calf through a gate. You didn't holler or wave your arms. You just were there in front of the calf every time it got the idea of going somewhere else.

He knew the kid had come to the creek to watch. He

knew the kid's heart splintered when he saw how easily Little Si ran Jewel down. He knew the kid suffered when he saw how the gray filly fought the rope, but that did not last long. She was behaving herself, holding her head to one side so she wouldn't step on those rope hackamore reins, when he brought her back across the creek.

"Isn't she beautiful?" the kid breathed.

"Monte, she's just about worthless."

"*Wha-a-at?*"

"She's beautiful, all right, because she's yours, you won her fair and square, you done the impossible and walked her down and tamed her before you ever laid a hand on her. But part of horsemanship, Monte, is judging a horse—and you don't lay a hand on her for that, either."

He got down to the ground again and pointed out Jewel's many defects. He like to broke the kid's heart.

But then he said, "What we're going to do, Monte, is wait a year until she has made her growth, and then breed her to Little Si. There's a gray horse somewhere in his line because every now and then, he throws a gray foal. It's ten to one he'll get one on her for you, and then you'll have yourself a horse! That don't mean you've got to think any less of Jewel. Think of it this way. You and me is going to be friends, and anybody in this county will tell you that Alec Pitman is a quarrelsome, overbearing, tightwad bastard, and so forth. But even if I am, I still expect you to be loyal to me because we're friends."

"One of my troubles," the kid burst out, "is that I don't make friends easily."

Alex nodded. "I can well believe that, but a few *good* friends beats a lot of half-assed ones every time. You made friends with Jewel, and she may not be much of a horse but she's still a lot better than most human beings I know. What's that around your neck?"

The kid fingered the medal hanging from a gold chain. "St. Jude," he said.

"Catholic?"

"Yes."

"They's a Catholic church here, not a short ride by no means, but the priest and me is pretty good friends. Father Leo Lagasse. But what we need right now is some breakfast."

The kid did not reply, but it was plain that he was half starved. He mounted his gray two-year-old and mastered her nicely despite her terror of the stud and the lack of a bit in her mouth. By the time they had got back to the Broken T, Alec had learned all he wanted or needed to know about the kid. Not his name, not his address, not his age, not the reason he had run away from home. Nothing like that.

What he learned was that here was a lost and lonesome kid who had been working heart and soul and mind at one thing for what was a long time in a kid's life. Now he had it, and he didn't know what to do next, or even what to want next. He *wanted* to be taken in hand and given a goal, work to do, something to think about, a new dream. He needed to learn the important lesson that the end of a chapter was not the end of the book. You just turned the page.

Edie had hooked up a team to the wagon and pulled the bodies of Paul and Reva Trotter into the hay shed, closing its door and then the gate behind them. She looked like she'd been whipped. She always took things hard and never knew how to start herself bouncing back from sadness.

"Ma," Alec said, sliding off Little Si, "here's a runaway kid I'm going to put to work. He goes by the name of Monte and he's half starved. After he's been fed, I'm going to give him a horse and a saddle and a bridle and send him over to help Dave Conn dig Esther Butterworth's well."

Edie looked at the kid on his two-bit horse with the rope hackamore. "I declare, Alec," she said. "He needs pants and a shirt and boots, too."

"Yes, I thought you could fit him out from the store chest."

They had to keep clothing to sell to the men, and Ma had it all locked in a huge chest in the house. She did not ask why he was hiring a runaway boy to help Dave Conn dig a well for the Widow Butterworth. She beat up some pancakes and fried some bacon and eggs, and while the kid ate she sized him up and then went and brought him clothing from the chest.

"You're in luck, Monte," she said. "I had all your sizes, I think. There's winter underwear there, too, and socks and a jacket."

The kid started to thank her and then suddenly remembered. "My shotgun!" he cried. "I left it back there in my dugout."

"And it's all you own," said Alec, who was having a second breakfast, too. Not as much as the kid, though. You could feed a haying crew cheaper than you could this youngster.

"Yes."

"Plenty of time to get your shotgun later. Now, I'm going to draw you a map of how to get to this lady's place, and I don't want you to stop and talk to anybody if you can get out of it. She'll put you up there until her well is down and cased. You'll make some muscles before you're through cranking the windlass. Then I'll have some colts for you to break."

"What about Jewel?"

"I'll keep her in the small corral. Do her good to miss you awhile. Do you good, too."

The grub made the difference. With a full belly on him, the kid had already lost some of the intensity that made the whole world just a place for him to follow the gray filly. He said all right and reached for more pancakes, and Ma got tears in her eyes to see him eat. She could forgive a young fellow a lot of things if he was a good eater.

Alec sent him off after breakfast on one of the best horses he owned, a five-year-old gelding with lots of ginger and a sensitive mouth. The kid's eyes were as big as muskmelons after he had tried the horse for a romp across the yard. Alec handed him a sealed envelope.

"You give the lady this note," he said, "and remember, she don't know it but you're going to be the man of the house there for a while. She needs taking care of, and this Dave Conn is no good. Don't let him get you into trouble. Use your head as well as you did with the gray horse, and remember—if you need me, the horse you're on can outrun anything Dave owns."

"Yes, sir."

The kid could hardly wait to be on the road with the splendid bay under him. The note he carried said:

Dear Esther: This lad is Monte. He'll work the windlass for Dave, and you don't need to tell Dave he come from me. He's just some boy you hired and Dave won't be jealous. I'll get your

*hay in soon as Max catches these murderers and
I can have my men back.*

Lovingly, Alec.

He did not realize that he had written "lovingly" until the kid was miles away. It had just popped out. This damn murder had him all upset, too. Everybody had the dismals, seemed like.

CHAPTER ELEVEN

The murderers vanished from the face of the earth.

Mose sent a man fogging back as hard as it was safe to run a horse with a message for Alec late that night. They had lost the trail, picked up the trail, lost it and picked it up again and again. When they lost it the last time, about noon, Max and Mose had decided to split the posse. Max took four men and Mose three.

Max could not believe two fugitives who were trying to make time would long stick to the timber. He headed north by west, betting he would pick up the trail in more open country. He would look for the ashes of campfires, for the bones of game, for tracks where horses had been watered. He had Tango Tangerus with him, and Tango was a fair tracker.

Old stubborn Mose was betting that the two would prefer the concealment of trees. That they did not have the horses to make a run for it. That they were heading for Johnson County and the Powder River, and if he was wrong, why, he was just wrong.

"He figgers," said the man who brought the news, "that these two could've been some of the gunmen hired for the Johnson County War. There was some of the God-damnedest riffraff in the world found jobs up there then, and they like to never got rid of them. Will Foutz has been through there, and he's with Mose. The sheriff thinks Mose is loony."

"I don't," said Alec. "What does Mose expect of me?"

"A fresh horse for me," said the man, "and all the forty-five ammunition you can spare, and some cash money. He figgers it this way, Alec. Them two must've been flat-ass broke to try something like that, and they sure didn't get away with much from the Trotters. They'll have to steal their grub, and Mose wants to be able to buy and spend freely. His idee is, you take people on the wrong side of the law, the quickest way to break up friendships is to spread around the cash money."

"You tell Mose," said Alec, "that I think he's using his head for something besides candlewicks, but don't go blundering into them and getting somebody shot all to hell. You better bait up now, and then catch a few hours' sleep."

"Oh hell, give me some saddle grub and I'm on my way."

"Now, nobody expects you to kill yourself on this job."

"Tell that to Paul and Reva."

Yes-sirree-bob, I've got myself some good men on this crew, Alec told himself as the man left on a fresh horse. . . . Grayson Figg arrived with his black wagon with the black curtains, attended by his son-in-law, Bob Kirk, and three of Bob's friends.

"Your posse is miles away by now, miles away!" Dr. Figg grumbled. "What do you expect of Bob?"

"I'll tell you what I expect," Alec said, deciding it was time to crack the whip a little. "They ain't going to blunder into those fellows sitting around and swapping lies beside a campfire. They're going to have to run them down and it may take days. I expect Bob and these boys to feed here, and take up the trail soon as they can. Watch for these two bastards in case they slip past both Max and Mose, and double back. Catch up with Mose and do what any man would do that calls himself a man—help catch these killers."

"Makes sense," said Bob Kirk, which was about as much as he ever had to say about anything.

Edie and Duke hurried up a meal. Figg insisted that Alec hook up a team and drag the wagon back into the sunlight while he examined the bodies, and then he wanted a witness for the examination. It made Alec sick to think about it, but Doc had checked the bet to him and he had it to do.

Paul had been battered up a little, but he had not died from torture. A shot in the belly had put him out of his misery. "He didn't die instantly," Figg said, "but if it was a forty-five, his whole system would be enervated by shock. He would be unconscious as he bled to death. Relatively merciful death, don't you see?"

"I see," Alec gagged.

"But poor Reva died by inches. I'm going to insist that Max hold an inquest, and I want you to be able to testify as a witness. Max—God knows when that idiot will be back, and these people have got to be buried promptly and decently. It won't be necessary to operate, but I want to show you—"

After Figg had left with the two bodies in his hearse, after writing up his notes like the plodding, methodical old grouch that he was and having Alec initial them, Alec went into the house and poured himself a drink. A big one. A water glass, two-thirds full.

"What's the matter with you?" Duke asked, coming into the room as Alec tossed back about half of the drink.

"Nothing," said Alec. "Shut up, will you?"

His mother came into the room, too. "I think you and Duke had better butcher a beef," she said. "If we're going to feed everybody that comes through, I'm going to—what's the matter with you?"

"Nothing," Alec snarled.

His mother fitted her hand over her chin and cheek, little finger along her cheek as she cocked her head. "Was it pretty bad?" she asked softly.

"Ma," he said, "let me alone, will you?"

"I saw the two of you there at the wagon. Believe me, I didn't—"

"Will you for *Christ's* sake let me alone?"

"After I say this one thing, Alec. If you're going to be a leader in your community, your father used to say, you're going to get more dirty jobs than honors. You have to be a lawyer with the lawyers, a politician with the politicians, a merchant with the merchants, he always said. And I guess a doctor with the doctors. It's no comfort, I know, but it goes with being Alec Pitman."

He thought wildly about Monte, young Master Nameless, who had not had to be or do any of these things. All he had to do was what he wanted to do, walk down a wild horse.

"I guess so," he said, with more self-control than he had thought he had in him.

Ma went out. Duke got out his butchering knives, and Alec hastily tossed down the rest of his drink as Duke began *whick-whick-whicking* them on his butcher's steel. The whiskey hit bottom and just seemed to evaporate. He might as well have drunk spring water. Duke picked up his knives and the big pack of folded squares of heavy muslin in which he wrapped beef. This time of year it did not need ice. He left the windows of his storeroom open and the room stayed cold enough for it to keep.

"I'm ready whenever you are, Alec."

Alec followed him to the fattening pen, where five culls had been putting on the fat on all the barley they could eat. One of Duke's prerogatives was to select the one they would butcher. He chose a leggy heifer, probably a good two years old. Sterile, or she would have been carrying a calf by now. He got a rope around her neck and snubbed it around the corner post of the pen.

They were pretty good at this, Alec and Duke. Alec used the ball end of a six-pound ball-peen hammer to stun the critter with, and Duke held his knife to stick it as it fell. Usually, that is.

Alec's hands were slimy with sweat as he picked up the hammer. "Duke," he said, "I can't do it."

"Sure," said Duke. "Go have yourself another drink. You look like hell."

"Another drink won't do me any good. Know what I'd like to do?"

"Hold somebody by the throat and pound his face in?"

"Yes." *And I know whose, too.* . . .

"Go on, I can take care of this."

"Oh, hell." Alec wiped his hands on his pants and picked up the hammer. "I never yet asked any man to do a job I couldn't do myself."

CHAPTER TWELVE

There was a town—not really a town, actually—that used to be called St. Catherine's Corner, a Roman Catholic church that had been built when the two roads were just two trails, and a store and an unofficial country postmaster. One of the partners in the store rode in twice a week to pick up the mail, and he had a sort of crush on Mrs. Butterworth. He always picked her mail up too, and went out of his way to deliver it.

"I guess you heard about Paul and Reva Trotter," he said, as he handed her her letters.

"No, what about them?"

He told her what had happened, and a lot that had not happened. Nobody ever knew how all these wild stories got around so fast in such an empty country, but they sure did.

"I haven't been away from the house," Esther said, feeling faint, "and no one has been here except Alec Pitman, yesterday afternoon. Oh dear, I wonder if there's anything I can do to help?"

"Just keep a gun loaded and watch out for strangers," the mail rider said. "You sure shouldn't ought to be living alone here."

"Oh, I'm all right!" she said.

But she was not all right. She was lonesomer than she had ever been in her life, and scared witless. She went into the house and got down the twenty-bore shotgun she kept on the kitchen wall. She always kept it loaded, and it was loaded today.

But the only time she had ever felt the need of it had been a few days ago, when that fellow stopped for a drink of water and to hit her up for a job. A job, her foot. He was a vicious, degenerate old man, and what he wanted was to know that she was alone in the house, and defenseless.

She had talked to him through the open door of the kitchen. "Help yourself to a drink down at the windmill," she said. "There's a gourd dipper there. You can't miss it."

His shabby clothing and his sorry horse went with his greasy, unshaven face. Here was one of God's own misfits if she had ever seen one. He had dismounted, but he was in no hurry to go get his drink.

"I see you're digging a well," he said, leering. "I'm an old well digger. Need a good man?"

"No."

"Fall's going to be on you soon, and then winter. All that work'll be wasted if your well ain't finished by the time the snow flies," he reminded her, leering.

"Do you want a drink or don't you?"

"Yes, but I hate drinking out of a gourd. Have you got a cup you could let me have?" he asked, leering.

"I've got this," she said, reaching around to take the twenty-gauge from its pegs on the wall. She let him see her pull back the hammer. "It's loaded, it's always loaded just in case somebody like you comes along, and I've killed prairie chickens by the hundreds with it, if you take my meaning."

"Great heavens, ma'am, don't point that thing at me!"

the man cried. "I didn't mean nothing. All I want is a drink of water."

"Just a minute," she snapped at him. "Don't you get on that horse yet! What's your name?"

"Why do you want my name?"

"I want to give it to the sheriff."

"The sheriff already knows me," he said, his voice rising in alarm. "You mean Sheriff Max Maddox. Why, me and him is old friends! I just sold him a fine team and buggy. You can ask him about me."

"What's your name, God damn you?"

He was so scared he gaped, he gasped, he seemed to be choking for air. "Bill Hazelwood," he said.

"Get the hell off my place and never let me catch you on it again."

"Yes, ma'am! But you misunderstood me, ma'am. All I wanted was a drink of water."

He mounted, and flogged his sorry old horse back to the county road, and Esther carried the shotgun with her as she went to the north window to watch. He headed north. He could be going to the Bar X or the Broken T, or right on past both.

This had happened several times since the death of her husband, but she had never had to threaten a would-be intruder with the shotgun before. A show of furious bravado had sufficed—and indeed she had felt no fear until that specimen had appeared the other day. Something about him just chilled her.

She looked down at Wolf and Robber, big dogs, vicious-looking dogs, but worthless as watchdogs. She was too easy on them, Alec Pitman said. But she could not bring herself to chain them and do the other things necessary to make them distrust strangers. Maybe, she thought, if she separated them it would help. Make one stay outside, keep the other in the house. Let them take turns.

"You, Wolf, you loafer, out you go," she said. "No, Robber, you stay here."

Wolf, a big, woolly dog, brown and black and white, grinned and showed his inch-long fangs as she let him out the door. She had to slam it on Robber's nose. She had no idea what kind of dog Wolf was, but Robber was mostly bull mastiff, she was sure.

They were uneasy at being separated. She could hear Wolf loping around the house and sniffing at both doors, wondering where his chum was. She finished her morning housework and then hated to go outside. In the first place, Dave Conn had not been around for a couple of days, and the way she felt now, she would just as soon he never came back. A lot of what Alec felt about Dave had to be plain old jealousy, but it confirmed an uneasiness she had been unwilling to admit was in her before.

She heard Wolf barking his fool head off, a deep, hoarse, angry bark. Robber went crazy, trying to get out. Separating them had done the trick. She took down the shotgun and pushed Robber back with the butt of it as she went out the kitchen door.

There was a long, limber-looking, yellow-haired kid sitting on one of Alec Pitman's Broken T horses, waiting for somebody to call off the dog. Wolf was being very brave. The hair stood up on the back of his neck, and he faced the horse and rider and stopped barking as she came out.

"Looking for someone?" she asked.

"Yes, ma'am," he said. "For Mrs. Butterworth, with a note from Mr. Pitman." He held up the envelope.

"Very well," she said. "Get down and bring it to me."

She spoke sharply to Wolf, who backed up and stood

beside her, snarling silently. The kid dismounted and came toward her. He knew how to handle dogs, all right. He simply paid no attention to Wolf, and on the other hand, made no sudden motions toward her. He held out the envelope at arm's length and then stepped back two steps.

She grounded the shotgun and tore the envelope open. At first she thought, Ha, old Mister Fix-it, he's just got to command, hasn't he? Do this, do that. . . . Then she came to that "lovingly," and her heart swooped like a flight of ducks coming down on a pond in the autumn twilight. She looked the boy over and liked him.

"So you're Monte," she said, smiling.

"Well, yes," he said.

"No last name?" He did not answer, but if a last name were important, Alec would have said so in his letter. "Well," she continued, still smiling, "I can't afford to pay very much, Monte, but I can surely use some help."

"Mr. Pitman will pay me. He said that I'll be working for him, ma'am."

"He did, did he? What kind of work will you be doing for him?"

"Breaking colts, ma'am."

"Oh," she cried, "are you the boy who walked down the wild gray filly? Oh, Alec told me about you. That was just splendid!"

The boy dropped his gaze to the ground. "Yes, ma'am, that was I."

"Where is the gray?"

"In her own corral at Mr. Pitman's place. I get to keep her, he said. He bought her for me and is going to let me work it out."

"Come into the house and tell me about it. Put your

horse in the corral and hang your saddle under the roof yonder. Could you eat something this time of day? But of course, a growing boy can always eat!"

"Ma'am, Mr. Pitman said I was supposed to help dig your well."

Suddenly she felt very lighthearted. She put her arm around the boy and gave him a squeeze. "The man you're supposed to help hasn't showed up yet. Take care of your horse and then, do you see that basket? Bring in a basket of cobs for the kitchen fire, and I'll fix us something to eat."

She went inside, keeping Wolf out and Robber in. When the boy came to the door with the basket of corncobs, he had only to speak to the dogs and they obeyed. He was, she saw, like Alec in one way—he had a natural gift of command that she lacked.

She warmed up some leftover navy bean soup and toasted some stale bread in the oven. It felt like a party when they sat down together.

"How far have you gone in school, Monte?"

"I would rather not say anything about myself, ma'am. I have put all that behind me forever."

"You're well educated for one so young, and I'm not guessing about that. I taught school, you know. Now I'm just a farmer-lady. I don't talk to anyone with an education, I have no time to read, and I'm growing uncouth and ignorant."

"I should think you would be afraid to live alone here, ma'am."

"I never was before, but I am now."

"You mean since the murders."

"Really, even before that. There was a man who

stopped here the other day who gave me nightmares. Can you shoot a twenty-gauge shotgun?"

"Oh yes, I'm a good wing shot, ma'am."

"Oh, good! I'll tell you what this fellow looked like, and if he turns up here again, he's to be greeted at gunpoint."

She described the man who had leered at her so threateningly. She did not notice that Monte stopped eating to squint at her with his mouth open.

"Just one man?" he asked when she had finished. "Not two?"

"Monte, there could be only one man as ugly and disreputable-looking as this one. I even know his name, or what he *said* was his name. Bill Hazelwood."

"No, ma'am," Monte said. "There is another one even worse, by the name of Ezra Tully, and they're the ones that murdered those people."

"How do you know that?" she whispered, when she could get any sound at all out.

For a second or two he seemed unwilling to talk about it, but once he made up his mind, he held nothing back. It had made such an impression on him that he could recall every word spoken. He made her see the desperate ferocity of that moment when Ezra had fallen on Haze to cut his bad tooth out or cut his throat, and it didn't much matter which. Perhaps the tooth had been aching when Bill Hazelwood stopped here the other day. In a way, the thought made her a party to the whole thing.

"Did you tell Alec about this?"

"No, ma'am, I didn't have a chance."

"Oh dear, I wish you had!"

"He was so busy. His mother, Mrs. Pitman—"

"No, her name is Mrs. Shook, but she is his mother."

"She was upset about having the two bodies there, and

he had so much on his mind. Anyway, Mrs. Butterworth, those two are fugitives. We're not going to see them around here. All of Mr. Pitman's men are out chasing them with the sheriff."

"All the same," she said, "I want to get word to Alec some way that I want to see him, but we mustn't let Dave Conn know."

"That's what Mr. Pitman said."

"I'll have to think about this. Finish your soup and go out and start shoveling some of that dirt farther back from the hole. I know that has to be done. And remember, if Dave shows up, you just dropped in here and I hired you."

"Yes, ma'am, Mr. Pitman explained all that."

Monte went out and got to work on the pile of dirt, willingly if not very skillfully. Esther realized that she was letting Alec take charge in a way she would not have tolerated as late as twenty-four hours ago, but only a fool would be stubborn about changing when circumstances changed. She felt much, much better with Monte here.

She heard Wolf barking, and then Dave Conn's voice. She went to the kitchen window and stood back where she could not be seen. Dave got off his horse and took a couple of kicks at the dog. At least he could call it by name, and Wolf decided finally to recognize him.

"Who are you, kid?" Dave growled. Monte told him. "You mean," Dave went on, "you just rode in here on a Broken T horse, a perfect stranger, and she hired you?"

(Oh dear, that's something none of us thought about! Alec's horse is a giveaway. . . .)

"He's got my horse," Monte said, "so I think I have a right to one of his."

"Your horse? What horse is that?"

"My little gray two-year-old filly."

"You the friend he bought that range colt of mine for?"

"I thought I was his friend. He's got the horse locked up in a pen, and he says I've got to work for him until I've paid it out. If he can just take my horse away from me, I can take one of his."

What a gifted little liar the boy was! Esther listened a little longer.

"You've got Pitman figgered out," Dave said. "The high-and-mighty son of a bitch don't even know that slavery was outlawed, but a good way to get into trouble is to steal somebody's horse."

Esther opened the door. "Hello, Dave," she said. "I see you've met my helper."

"Yes, but you know what's going to happen if Alec Pitman finds out the horse this brat stole is here."

"I'll take care of Alec, never fear," she said serenely. "Monte's going to help us with the well. I shan't worry about Alec's horse, and I don't want Monte worried about it, either. I shall charge Alec for boarding his horse, if I take the notion."

"Hey, that's sense!"

From the window, she saw Dave show Monte how to work the windlass to lower the big wooden bucket, and how to crank it back up and dump it. They lowered it again, and Dave locked the pawl on the ratchet, took hold of the rope, and slid down out of sight.

It took Monte only a few minutes to get onto the work, to the point where he was really better at it than Esther had ever been. But with a clarity of inner perception that she had lacked before, she now wished heartily that she had never let Dave start the well. It was a mistake to owe him anything, she knew that now.

CHAPTER THIRTEEN

The man who got off the westbound train had three fine pigskin bags and carried a tailored wool overcoat with a caracul collar. He took the Jessup Hotel's station wagon to the hotel and signed up for one of the two best rooms: Melvin L. Devlin, of Boston, Massachusetts. He proffered his card, which identified him as a partner in Crane, Vanderlip, Devlin and Crane, attorneys at law, to to the clerk.

"What would be a good time to talk to your sheriff?" he asked.

"By golly, just at this moment that's a hard question to answer," the clerk replied. "There was a kind of a nasty murder here yesterday, and he's out with a posse trying to pick up the trail."

"Oh? You have such an attractive, peaceful community here, it's hard to believe a murder could have been committed, really."

He was a good-looking, middle-aged man with a pair of sharp eyes under bushy, brindle eyebrows and a pleasant smile under a big red mustache. He had ridden the train in a three-piece suit that had stood travel well. His hat—the clerk had learned to judge men by their hats—was an expensive one that was used to good care.

A rich man, a decisive man, a man used to big affairs, and a man to whom good manners were not an affectation. This Mr. Melvin L. Devlin liked people, poor ones as well as rich ones, and he was genuinely interested in them. Thus the judgment of the clerk, who was also the assistant manager.

The clerk told Mr. Devlin about the murder of Paul and Reva Trotter. "That's shockingly sad," said Devlin. "We expect things like that in the big city, but I imagine everyone here will be in mourning."

"That's right, sir."

"Well, I'll just have to wait until your sheriff returns. He's the Honorable Maxwell Maddox, isn't he?"

The clerk had never heard old Max called either "honorable" or "Maxwell," but he agreed that Mr. Devlin had the right party. Mr. Devlin ordered a bath, and came down to supper in the dining room in another suit. He asked about someone to wash some shirts and underwear for him, and then tipped the bellhop fifty cents to take the bundle of laundry to the place.

A man who traveled first-class, that was plain. A man who tipped generously but not lavishly. A man used to far better food than the Jessup provided, but who ate what was there with enjoyment and without complaint.

Mr. Devlin spent the evening in two saloons, buying the beer, drinking and talking very little, but listening with an attentive smile. He retired about eleven and was up, freshly shaven and in still another suit, by seven. After breakfast, he stopped at the hotel desk and unfolded a large piece of white butcher paper.

"Here's a map someone was kind enough to make for me," he said. "Last night I felt I was familiar with it but I wish you would freshen my perspective."

The clerk studied the map. "Who drawed this for you, sir? It's a good one, but his writing ain't very plain, is it?"

"I don't know whether it's his writing or my reading."

The clerk pointed out the main roads, warning Mr. Devlin that some of them were not going to look like much to a man used to paved streets. Mr. Devlin said that he did a great deal of business in rural areas and was used to country roads.

"Now, if you take this fork to the northeast, that brings you to the Broken T. But halfway there you'll see another fork to your right that leads to the Bar X. Or you can start from town here and take this fork to what used to be homestead country, and you'll pass the Four Plus and then the Bar X and then you hit the Broken T," the clerk said.

"A more roundabout way," said Mr. Devlin.

"Yes."

"Are any of these properties for sale?"

"Well, you keep hearing that the Bar X could be bought, but they been saying that for years."

Mr. Devlin tapped the map. "Go back to this crossroads. Suppose, instead of taking the northeast fork, you take the other one. What's this place he has marked here?"

"That's Trotter's Corner. That's where those two people were murdered."

"I see. Suppose, though, you take this road to the north before you come to Trotter's Corner—where does it lead?"

"St. Catherine's Corner. Or I reckon they just call it St. Catherine's around here now. They's a Catholic church there, and not much else. Someday it could be quite a town, though."

Mr. Devlin passed his hand across part of the map. "What's all this country like?"

"Beautiful country, Mr. Devlin. Most of that is Broken T range, and nobody takes better care of land than Alec Pitman. There's bluestem grass up to your knees there, and creeks full of trout and bass."

"I don't suppose the Broken T is for sale?"

"Mr. Devlin," the clerk said, in a shocked voice, "Alec don't *sell* land, he *buys* it."

"He's centrally located. If I were to presume to ask to spend the night there—?"

"You won't get a chance to ask. Alec and his mother will rope you and tie you. Fine people, fine people!"

Mr. Devlin engaged his room for a week, hired the best team and buggy from the livery stable, and set out with only one small valise shortly after breakfast. He took the road past the Four Plus, and gave it only a passing glance. There were a few horses in the corrals, and a milk cow, but he saw no signs of human life about the place and there was a big, ugly dog that came out to view his rig challengingly.

From the top of a grade nearly a mile away, he looked back. He could see someone working back of the house, someone who had been concealed by the house when he passed it. Hard to tell what was going on, but there seemed to be a pile of fresh dirt. Digging a well, maybe.

He had had a lunch packed for him, and he finished eating it just as he came to the pair of ruts that led to the Bar X. He had been warned about the gates. He got down and opened this one, led his team through, and closed it behind him. He got back into the buggy and drove on.

In another half hour, taking it easy, he came to the drab little set of buildings. A man came out to meet him, his hat on the back of his head and his hands in his pockets. He looked like a nice, easygoing old fellow and he had a friendly grin.

"Hidy, hidy," he said. "Welcome to the dangedest old lonesome cow ranch in the world. My name is Buchert, James A. Buchert, only mostly I'm called 'Buck' as you can well imagine."

Devlin got down, identified himself by his card, and shook hands. Buck insisted on tying the team for him, and he would have watered them had not Devlin managed to get a word in edgewise. "No, I forded a little creek not far back, and I let their checkreins down before we went into it so they could drink."

"Ain't everybody dressed like you are that knows how to take care of a team that way," said Buck.

"I grew up on a rocky old Massachusetts farm, and I haven't forgotten much."

"Say, now! I had an uncle married a woman from Massachusetts."

Turned out that Mr. Devlin had not known Sophia Halstead, but he had known other Halsteads in the Fall River area. They sat on the front porch and talked, Buck luxuriating in the fine cigar that Mr. Devlin gave him.

"I've thought of selling, yes, I have," Buck said, "but I'm mixed up in a kind of mess, a deal I've got with a sharecrop manager. I don't know how the *hell* I let myself get talked into this deal. I didn't like the man then and I don't like him now, but he made it sound *so* good! I'd lost my wife, see, and I just couldn't seem to get caught up with anything. Just no reason to work, seemed like. He was going to take care of everything, all I had to do was feed us and do the chores."

"What kind of profit split?" Mr. Devlin asked.

"I thought ten per cent, but no, he says now it was ten

per cent *after* he figgered himself wages for the time he put in."

"What wages?"

"Well, *he* says fifty dollars a month except in haying time, when it's a hundred, and *I* never heard of nobody getting fifty a month for no more than he does around here. The haying season, he said, is two and a half months, and that's all right if you've got that much hay to put up. But I've got one mowing machine and one side-delivery rake and one buck, and I generally borry a stacker from Alec Pitman. So far this year—"

Buck turned and tapped Devlin on the wrist to emphasize what he was saying: "So far this year he ain't put up *one single ton* of hay. He's spent all his time digging a well for a lady lives down the road yander. But I bet you in his reckoning, I owe him haying wages."

"How much do you think his reckoning would come to altogether, in unpaid wages?"

Buck held his head in his hands. "I bet you it's over fifteen hundred dollars."

"Why don't you let me see the agreement? I'm a lawyer, you know."

"We didn't write nothing down. We just shook hands on it. I must've been insane!"

"It's almost impossible to enforce an oral contract in court without clear evidence of intent by both parties, or reliable witnesses, or both. Just tell him to go to the devil and let him sue you."

Buck shuddered. "I wouldn't dare. People would laugh if I said this, but that man's a killer. They don't know him like I do. I don't dare leave my place, because I'll never get back on it if I do. I don't dare stay here because he'll kill me, I know that, someday he'll kill me and I don't care if you do laugh at me, that's the truth."

"Why don't you dare leave your place?"

"Because he'd never let me back on."

"Nonsense! If you're in fear of your life, you have a right to leave, and a right to the court's protection when you return. Isn't there someplace you can go and live in safety with friends, while a lawyer gets a writ from the court?"

"Oh yes, I could stay with Alec Pitman."

"Is your judge honest? Is there a lawyer who would not be intimidated by this man?"

"Yes, sure, but—"

"No buts, Mr. Buchert. I want to drop in on Mr. Pitman and see if I can presume to spend a few days with him. You might be my ambassador, eh? My team has rested. Get your things together and let's go, shall we?"

Buck actually got tears in his eyes. "It's the hand of God," he said. "I'm an old man and I never was a fighting man. You don't know what it is not to have a moment's peace on your own place!"

Alec Pitman was in his shop, shaping some new spokes just in case he might need to rebuild a wheel someday. It was a neat, orderly shop, his ironworking gear in one end, his woodworking tools in the other, his harness repair bench along the wall next to the windows. He saw the buggy come into the yard and recognized it as the livery stable's rig.

He went out to meet it and saw Buck Buchert and a well-dressed stranger. He was in the habit of sizing up a man fast, and before Melvin L. Devlin gave his name,

Alec had him pegged as a man of affairs and one hell of a good poker player.

"I'm shopping for ranch property," the stranger said, "and I've been to see Mr. Buchert. Everyone says I may take the liberty of imposing myself on you for a few days as a guest, and Mr. Buchert substantiates that."

Alec went cold at the thought of someone else getting his hands on the Bar X, but he was not a bad poker player himself. "We're in an uproar here," he said, "because my whole crew is out trying to track down a couple of murderers. But if you can put up with us, it would be a pleasure to have you, sir."

"I'd like to hole up with you myself," Buck quavered, with an apologetic smile. "Mr. Devlin's a lawyer, and he says I don't have to be afraid Dave Conn can keep me off my own land. And I'm sure as the dickens scared to stay on it!"

Alec narrowed his eyes. "Scared of Dave?"

"Oh, say! You ain't going to believe it, Alec, but that fella has just got me buffaloed. He—he treats me like a dog in my own house, and I know, I just *know*, that if I sass him back he'll beat me half to death. I can't explain, but that man is a killer and I know it!"

"You don't have to explain, Buck," said Alec. "Let's go in and ask Ma to make the beds in a couple of bedrooms, and then I'll put up your horses."

"If—if Dave comes here looking for me, what are you going to say?"

"You let me worry about that, Buck. I won't say anything I ain't wanted to say for some time."

CHAPTER FOURTEEN

Mose returned before dark, leading the entire posse. Sheriff Max Maddox was with it, but there was no question about it, he had conceded leadership to Mose.

They were all tired, hungry, and in the same vile temper. Edie had served one supper for Alec, Buck, and Devlin, but she had lived here too long to be unprepared for this. No more than Alec had she expected the posse to catch up with the murderers of Paul and Reva Trotter.

Sheriff Maddox was exhausted. After eating, he went straight to bed in the bunkhouse and went instantly to sleep. He had not inquired about his new buggy team, to Alec a sure sign that his ownership of them was weighing more heavily than ever on him. This, more than the physically arduous chase, was what had tired him out.

And well it might. Max might get away with a bargain team and buggy, with a loan at the bank. But to be connected, however circuitously, with the two men who were suspects in the murder, was disaster. It meant the end of the road for him as sheriff.

Alec waited until they had all eaten, and then he gave Mose and Bob Kirk a furtive nod of the head that invited them to follow him. He led them out of the dining room, around the house, and in through the front door. He was not exactly surprised when Devlin came along. Devlin had come out, along with Buck, to greet the dispirited man hunters, and had sat at the table as they ate.

"I'm sure you want to talk about your pursuit, Mr. Pitman," he said, "and I beg your indulgence in letting me join you."

"Why?" Alec said, not discourteously, but still in a voice that extorted the truth.

"I'm an attorney," Devlin said, "and I'm not unfamiliar with criminal cases and the criminal mind. Perhaps I can help."

"That's not good enough, Mr. Devlin. I'd appreciate your help, sure enough. But I still wonder why the hell you offer it."

"Fair enough. I may have an interest in this matter. I have a client who may have, at least."

"So you're not just prospecting for a ranch to buy."

"That is correct. I am not interested in protecting your murderers. I will do anything I can to help apprehend them. I will help prosecute them when they are apprehended, and I'm a good prosecutor. I wish I could impose upon you to take me on faith and let me sit in with you."

The kid, that's what he's interested in, Alec thought. The kid that walked down the wild horse. . . . "All right with me, Mr. Devlin," he said. "We're not stupid folks out here, but by God we sure come up short on knowledge and education sometimes."

There was a snap in the air outside, and a dank chill in the little living room. He touched off the fire that was already laid, opening the dampers until he had it roaring. He closed the dampers down then, with the methodical air of a man who learned to do every job right, Devlin thought. When he took his place in the rocking chair near the door, everyone knew it was time to start talking.

"Alec," Mose said, "we ran into the tracks of two shod horses twice, when they crossed the creek. McMann's Creek the first time, and then the Little Beaver. Now, to me that means somebody is heading north to Converse County, and *that* means Johnson County next, and *that* means a couple of ring-tailed bastards who know they've got friends and a hidey."

Alec looked at Bob Kirk, who nodded. "You can't count on anything for sure," Bob said, "but if you've got to guess, that's your best guess. But then them tracks just vanished into thin air."

"Only thing that would do any good in that kind of grass would be a couple of bloodhounds, but you might as well wish for a regiment of cavalry."

Alec stirred in his chair. "I've thought many a time of getting a pair of bloodhounds and breeding a few litters. There's a fella in Logan County, Nebraska, that owns a pair of good trackers that he's always lending out to some sheriff or other. I think maybe I'll start looking for a pair."

"Yes," said Mose, "but they ain't going to do us no good now. The queer thing is, we gave up early this afternoon and started back. I know when I'm whipped. We taken a short cut through those willow brakes, you know where I mean?"

"Where Sandy Creek makes the hook, yes."

"Yes. And for nigh a hundred and fifty yards, here's the sign of two shod horses again, plain as the nose on your face."

"Same two horses?"

"Near as any of us could tell. Shod all around, that's for sure, and I ain't tracker enough to tell you any more. But what gits me, these tracks was heading *south!*"

"South?"

"Yes."

"I be blamed. If it's your fugitives, why are they turning around and heading straight back to where they come from?"

"It don't make sense, does it? We fanned out and follered them as fur as we could. Once you git out of the sand around them willows, you're back in grass and what you need is a pair of good bloodhounds. We wasted an hour and a half, two hours, trying to pick up that sign again."

"I be blamed!"

"Me and Bob figger there's three places they could be going. One, stick to the grass where they can kind of hide their sign until they come to the U.P. siding where they can catch a train, but what are they going to do with their horses if that's it? Two, back to town, and that's about the foolishest thing they could think of. Three, they could be heading here."

Alec nodded. "Or," he said, softly, "first to Paul and Reva's place to see if they missed anything, and then here, and then the Bar X."

"Well, I reckon so. We thought of leaving a couple of men at Trotter's, but we was all so damn hungry and tired, and does it seem likely to you that they'd go back there and try it again?"

"No. Did you mention any of this to Max?"

"Oh yes. All he said was, 'Oh lordy, oh my God, it ain't complicated enough,' and he 'peared to come plumb to the end of his rope. That old man just ain't as tough as he looks, for a big man."

Alec thought it over a long time. "I don't know what else you boys could've done. You rode hard and you used your heads, seems to me. Where'd you get back together with Max again?"

"He gave up before we did. They was resting their horses in that cottonwood grove when we catched up with them on the way home. Alec, that poor old man has just plain caved in. I didn't know he was that fond of Paul and Reva."

It was not Alec's place to sit in judgment. "Well," he said, "it's Max's first murder case. Let's see, if you cut across corners on the way back, you come close to St. Catherine's."

"Went right through it. Father Lagasse said to tell you hello."

"I s'pose he hadn't saw anything of two raunchy strangers lately."

"No, and I asked him."

"If I may ask a question, has *anyone* seen *any* strangers around here lately?" Devlin asked.

Now Alec was sure Devlin was on the track of Monte or whatever his real name was. He shook his head slowly. "Not that I know of. They come and they go, and this time of year a good, hustling rider usually has a job on somebody's roundup crew somewhere. Couple of months from now, you'll see lots of good men heading south. To winter in the Rio Valley, you know."

"You mentioned St. Catherine's. What is that?"

"A Catholic mission to the Indians that's a church now."

"When are their masses, do you know? I'm a Catholic myself and I've missed mass for three Sundays."

"Why," said Alec, "I believe every morning at eight, and on Sunday at seven, nine, and eleven. If you want to go in the morning, I can put you on a horse that will get you there faster than you ever could in a buggy. If you can ride, that is."

"Thank you, let me think about it. I love to ride, but how early would I have to start?"

"You should leave here by a quarter to seven, to get there by eight."

Devlin changed the subject. "You seem to have a fairly good description of your two fugitives. Do you mind telling me what they look like?"

Alec told him what Max Maddox had told him, but it was sadly lacking in detail. He watched Devlin closely, and it seemed to him that Devlin was greatly relieved to hear that both fugitives were men in their fifties, probably.

Well, Alec thought, that about cinches it. Monte wears a St. Jude's medal, and Devlin's interested in St. Catherine's. He's curious about strangers but he lost interest mighty fast when he found out that these two boogers wasn't neither one a kid. Let's just float along with him awhile. . . .

"Go to bed, both of you," he told Mose and Kirk. "You done fine. But then you two always turn in a job when you're asked, so I ain't surprised."

"Alec, I swear to God we all done the best we could," Mose said in a trembling voice. "We talked it over all the time and tried to think of the right thing to do, and we—"

He was about to launch off on one of those hollering fits of his; so Alec told them again to go to bed and sleep until the rumbling of their own empty guts woke them up. Mose and Bob Kirk went out, to go around the house to the bunkhouse. Devlin offered Alec a cigar, and the two sat smoking in the living room, growing sleepier as the crackling fire spread its glow and the fine, rich tobacco brought contentment. Alec knew that Devlin was dying to lead up to the subject of Monte and did not know how to go about it.

"If you're set on going to church tomorrow, Mr. Devlin," Alec said, "and I don't get stuck with something unexpected, I could take you there tomorrow."

"Why, are you R.C.?" Devlin asked.

"No. I ain't nothing. But me and Father Lagasse are good friends, and I ain't seen him in a long time."

He was sure Devlin was on the verge of saying something more, but changed his mind. "Let me think about it until morning. I'm afraid that once I get to bed, His Holiness himself couldn't get me out early."

"I kinda figgered that," Alec said.

He was worried sick about Esther Butterworth, yet he knew it would not be very smart to saddle up, and go down there this time of night. When he backed off and looked at things without letting worry distort his mind, he thought he could count on Esther's good sense and the wild kid's instinct and quick wit. One other thing bothered him. What was Dave Conn going to do when he got home and found Buck gone?

It was not time to force Dave's hand—not yet—and this might do it. But how could he have turned old Buck down? It was like a stud game. You let the cards fall, and if you started out trying to match up an ace in the hole to another ace, and found yourself with four of a suit after the fourth card dropped, you kept your wits about you. It was all right to think of catching a flush as well as another ace, but you did not have to go insane.

Mr. Devlin begged to be allowed to go to bed. Alec

went into the kitchen, where at eleven o'clock at night Ma had just taken a raisin pie out of the oven and was getting ready to serve it hot, with thick cream over it and fresh coffee beside it.

"Sit down and have some," she invited Alec, gaily. "James and I have been having a good old talk together."

"Mighty nice of y'all to take an old man in this way," said Buck. "First sociable evening I've had in two years, and a man gets so tired of his own bachelor kitchen, he just hates food."

"You just figger you're right in your own home here, Buck," Alec said. "Don't you talk about anybody taking you in."

"A person can always count on Alec," Edie said tearfully, putting a piece of hot pie in a bowl big enough to hold plenty of cream, and putting it before him. "Usually you can, anyway."

"But I'm afraid of tomorrow," Buck said.

"I ain't," said Alec.

"I'll have to face him sometime, though, and you don't."

"Don't let him bluff you. After he spends a lonesome night alone at the Bar X, trying to cipher out what's happened to you, he'll be an easier man to talk to. If it's been lonesome for two of you in that little house of yours, think about how it is for one," said Alec.

But Dave Conn was not spending a lonesome night alone at the Bar X.

CHAPTER FIFTEEN

Dave had never worked harder in his life, and Esther had never been more uneasy about him. She was torn two ways. Cranking the windlass and dumping that big dirt bucket were man-killing jobs, the way Dave was going at it, and she felt she ought to be out there giving Monte a hand. At the same time, though, she had a strong hunch that Dave Conn should be let alone today.

Not long after Dave arrived, a nester neighbor brought her a forequarter of young beef that he had butchered just that morning. "She was a fence jumper," he said disgustedly, "and she just ripped herself all to hell this time."

"You can't give me all this meat," she said.

"You've give us a sight more than that, Mrs. Butterworth. And I guess mostly I wanted to see how you's doing. It bothers Adelaide and me, you living alone here. These is bad times."

She expressed, cheerfully, her confidence in her dogs and her twenty-gauge. The neighbor warned her again before departing. She sliced off some thin shoulder chops for frying and decided to dry the rest of the carcass. She now had an excuse to remain in the house and watch through the window.

She threw the bones in her big soup pot and put them on to boil. She sliced the meat into long, narrow strips.

She built her greenwood fire under the drying rack that Lance had built, strung the meat on wire, and stretched the wire so the meat could cure in the smoke.

"Mrs. Butterworth, ma'am," Monte called to her, "Mr. Conn wants to talk with you."

Strange how much nerve it took to go to the edge of the hole and peer down. There stood Dave in a foot of water, looking up at her.

"I've made four feet and a half of bottom so far," he said.

"Oh, that's wonderful!"

"Can't go much further down without pumping, but so far I'm in sand with enough clay to cling. I wonder if you ain't about ready to feed a workingman."

"I've been waiting on you to say when," she replied contritely. "It'll take me just half an hour."

He smiled up at her. "Thanks," he said. "Come on, kid, heist this bucket up and let's make hole until she calls us."

She fried the chops and some potatoes, and opened a jar of last year's tomatoes and cooked them with dry bread with a sweet-and-sour flavor. She called to Monte that dinner was ready, and shortly Dave came up in the bucket. He had taken his boots and socks off and sent them up the moment the first water appeared. His old pants were soaked to above the knees and his bare feet looked obscenely pallid.

She heard his deep voice scolding Monte as they washed up at the bench just outside the kitchen door: "You make yourself right to home, don't you? Talk old silly Alec out of that gray filly, ride off on one of his, and now you're going to set down at the table with the workingman. Where'd you come from, kid?"

"Back East," Monte replied.

"Where back East?"

"I don't have to say."

She heard the grunt as Dave took a swipe at Monte with his hand, but when she got to the door they were five or six feet apart and she was sure Dave had missed. He was drying himself with the towel, his heavy growth of whiskers glistening like lacquered wire. He tossed the towel to Monte.

"It's ready whenever you two are," Esther said.

"Wash up good," Dave said.

He let Esther hold the screen door open for him and stalked into the house on his big bare feet. He saw the kitchen table set for three, and she knew he did not like it, she knew that it stirred ideas in him, aroused jealousies and stimulated ambitions, that he might not have dared to otherwise. He kept his face averted from her.

She showed him where to sit, and when Monte came in, she gave him a stool (she had only two chairs) that put him closer to her than to Dave. Dave did not like that either.

Her heart was pounding, pounding, pounding with terror, but she rose to the occasion. So far as either Dave or Monte could tell, she was sure, she had not a worry in the world. She ate lightly but she fed them well. She took note when Dave pushed his plate back and took his papers and tobacco from his shirt pocket. His fingers trembled.

"Let's get to work, kid," he said, when he had his cigarette going.

"Yes, sir," said Monte.

They went out together. She went to the window to watch. She saw Dave pick up the old shovel and start throwing dirt back from the edge of the hole. He was strong as a bull. He was making the dirt fly, exploding with power.

She knew what was going to happen. She moved the big teakettle back to the hot lids of the stove to start it seething again. She scraped the dishes, got out the two dishpans and a fresh bar of soap. There were only six left on the shelf in the pantry, she noted. She was a good soapmaker and she loved it and traded work with a couple of neighbors every January. She made their wives' soap and they did the spring disking for her.

She had a heavy maple potato masher that she also used to put in socks when she was darning them. It had a long handle with a small knob on one end and, on the other, a smoothly turned and shaped goose egg that had a knot in it, an eye-shaped knot. It was a little bigger than a goose egg and a little flatter on the end, and she had decided that it would make a good weapon of self-defense early in the lonely days after Lance's death.

She put it beside the dishpan and was washing dishes when Dave came into the room and closed the door behind him. She looked around and knew that there was no use pretending any longer. He was between her and the twenty-gauge. It was up to the potato masher.

"Esther," he said in a growling, gusty voice.

"Now what?" she said, narrowing her eyes and trying to intimidate him before he got started.

"I want that damn kid out of here."

"*You* want him out of here? Well, you've got your sass along today, haven't you?"

"He ain't going to sleep in the house with you. I may not be bright but I ain't a fool. I was teacher's pet myself once at the same age. By God, I can dig your well, I'm fit for that, I can work like a nigger and not ask you a cent for it, but when it comes to fun in the bedroom—"

She interrupted him: "What *are* you talking about? You just don't make sense."

He lost his head completely. Two quick steps—they were close to being jumps—brought him to where he could clutch her upper arms in his hands. "Jesus, Esther," he whimpered, "don't tantalize me like this. First that son of a bitch of a Pitman and then this baby-face kid."

He let go of her arms to embrace her. He pushed her head back with his own and found her mouth with his. He mumbled as he kissed her—loud, hungry, smacking kisses with his beard scratching her lips and cheeks raw and his arms almost breaking her back as one hand groped for her bottom.

She kept her head and let herself be overpowered, but her left hand found the maple potato masher and transferred it to her right. The damn fool had left her arms completely free. She grasped it by the small knob and twirled it behind his head, bringing the goose egg down on the back of his skull.

"Hey!" he shouted.

He was not badly hurt but he thought he had been attacked by a third party from behind. He saw his mistake too late. She swung the potato masher again and caught him on the side of the head—over the ear or on the temple, she neither knew nor cared which. I don't care if I've killed him, she told herself. . . .

The screen door opened and Monte came gliding in. She knew by the look on his face, by the way he reached for the shotgun, that he had been watching it all through the window. She shook her head at him. "No, no," she whispered. "Go on back to work. He'll be a good boy when he comes to. *If* he comes to. If he sees you here, he'll go crazy again."

"Ma'am, I don't like to—"

"Go back to work! Pretend you don't know anything. Get out of here, do you hear me?"

He aspired to be a hero but did not know how to go about it, but when she took the shotgun down from the pegs he surrendered and went out. Dave had not moved a muscle—not a twitch, not a blink of his eyes, not a visible breath. Esther dipped her hand in the water pail and wiped the nervous sweat from her face. She dried it with her apron, using only her left hand because she had the twenty in her right.

She began to be afraid when, after what seemed like an age, Dave still had not moved. Outside, she could hear the kid hacking away at that pile of moist, sandy dirt with the shovel. She took a dipper of water and let it trickle slowly over Dave's face and forehead.

In a moment he licked his lips and made a tiny, mewing sound. She trickled another dipper of water over him. He rolled over on his back, groaning. While he was still halfway between asleep and awake, she took another dipper of water in her left hand and slopped the whole thing in his face.

She stepped back so that when he said "Jesus!" and hoisted himself up to half-sitting, with most of his weight on his arms, the first thing he saw was her with the shotgun. She gave him plenty of time to pull his wandering mind back to the present. His hand went up to the big lump that was already rising on the left side of his head.

"You hit me," he said thickly.

"Yes," she said, "but it needn't go any farther, Dave. I appreciate all you've done, but I never want to see you on my place again. I'll pay you for your work, because I *will not* be obligated to a man who feels free to treat me as you tried to treat me. Now get out of here."

"Jesus," he said, "what did I do? I must've been crazy. I wouldn't harm a hair of your head, woman, you know that."

"We won't argue. Just go. Get on your horse and get out of here and never come back."

He got to his knees. "Please, you're just mad and I don't blame you, but you don't know what you're saying. You're all I care about in the world. I was out of my mind."

"Just go."

He stumbled to his feet and stood there reeling and pawing at the swelling on the side of his head. He might or might not have been out of his mind when he kissed her, but no question now, he was out of it completely, he did not know north from south. She could only hope to God that he did not make her shoot him right there in the kitchen.

He fell down when he tried to pick up his hat, but he clamped it on his head and pulled a chair to him and climbed up it to regain his feet again. "I'm sorry, Esther," he said. "From the bottom of my heart I'm sorry. I don't know what else I can say."

She almost, but not quite, felt a little sorry for him. He was still unsteady on his feet when he went out the door. She saw him reeling toward the open hole of the well. Monte retreated to the top of the dirt pile, taking the shovel with him.

"Got to make hole," Dave said. "Work your skinny little ass off, kid, that's what I'll do. Get the well dug. Got to dig us a well."

He threw the bucket into the well and watched the rope unwind on the windlass. He saw it go slack as the bucket hit the water at the bottom. He locked the pawl, grasped the rope with both hands, and launched himself downward.

He screamed when he hit bottom, as though he had cracked his shins or something on the bucket. Monte leaped for the windlass and began cranking. Dave's roar of rage came booming out of the deep hole so magnified in volume that it sounded like the echo of a cageful of roaring lions.

The bucket emerged from the well, empty. Monte caught it without locking the pawl and threw it up on the pile of dirt. He had to pick it up and throw it twice more before he had it over on the other side. Esther admired his quick wit when he took two quick half-hitches with the bight of the rope around one of her clothesline posts.

"We better get out of here, ma'am," he said. "Listen to him! He's a maniac. Let's go back to Mr. Pitman's place."

She thought of Edie Shook. "Oh no, never! We can't go away and leave him down there, Monte."

"We must, ma'am. What else can we do? You'll have to kill him if he gets out of there. Listen to him!"

She could not help listening. At first Dave had cursed Monte, but he knew now that she was up there at ground level. He was calling her names and promising what he would do to her when he got out. Mark her face up so she'd never show it in public again. Tear her clothes off and wire her wrists to her own chimney and go away and leave her straddling the ridgepole of her own house. And so on.

"There's some friend you could go to," Monte was insisting.

"Monte," she said, "I'm not going to throw myself on anyone's mercy in this. I won't be an object of ridicule or derision. I would rather kill him. I mean that."

"I know where you can hide as long as you want," he said. "We'll need some food, matches, and a candle or two if you have them. It's where I hid, ma'am, for over a month."

"All right," she said, handing him the shotgun. "Wait while I change into trousers. No, saddle your horse and saddle the gelding with the one white foot for me. He doesn't look like much but he's a goer."

He called after her to bring a blanket when she came. She emerged from the house a few minutes later, wearing a man's shirt and pants and carrying a gunnysack and a kettle. She yanked one wire from the meat-smoking rack down and slid the strips of meat from it into the kettle, which then went into the gunnysack.

On the way north, as the brief autumn twilight came on, he talked endlessly and with enthusiastic innocence about the gray filly, Jewel, and his long, patient pursuit of her. It was beautiful to hear, and it brought back forgotten dreams of her own childhood. She had been going to marry an actor, have a son like this one and call him Cosmo, hold Thursday *salons*, whatever they were, have her hand kissed by the Mayor of New York, the Italian Ambassador, God knew who else. So few people dreamed the right dreams or then lived up to them! But this boy had.

CHAPTER SIXTEEN

Haze was beginning to think that things were going better for him, finally. Or rather, he was not really thinking; he was too far gone for that. It was more of a feeling, a slight, inner resurgence of vitality just when he had given himself up for dead.

The important thing was that the country seemed like it had been full of mounted men all day, yet not one had spied him. Two different bunches of men that came together and sat chewing it over until he thought he'd go crazy with impatience.

But they had ridden off in one bunch at last, giving up the chase—oh yes, it was a chase, all right, and he and Ezra were what they were chasing! But now they had given up and Ezra was dead and it was no fault of Haze's that he was, and he had the son of a bitch's body along to prove it.

He followed the broad, careless trail left by the posse, shivering when he recognized the wagon road on which he and Ezra had approached Trotters' place and the worst luck he had ever had in his life. Any man was doomed that teamed up with somebody like Ezra, but if he brought Ezra's body in without a mark on it to show that *he* hadn't killed him, wouldn't that be proof that he hadn't killed the Trotters, either?

There was a right smart passel of lights and a lot of

noise up there at the Pitman place. Hungry as he was, cold as he was, Haze lost his nerve to ride up there and give himself up. He turned in the saddle and looked at Ezra's body, which he had tied securely across the saddle. He was a good man with a rope, he had to say that himself. *He* hadn't hurt that Trotter woman. The way he had tied her, she wasn't even very uncomfortable.

No, it was that son of a bitch of an Ezra who was to blame for everything. "He talked me into it," Haze would tell the sheriff, "and I didn't know he was going to rob them people until it was too late. He made me go with him at gunpoint. Why, I didn't even have a gun on me! If I had, do you think he'd've lived to die of heart failure? *You* wouldn't have to worry about hanging him because *I* would've shot him dead."

He had thrown away his own .45 and had Ezra's in his holster, and if that wouldn't convince them he didn't know what would. Only now wasn't the time. Them possemen would be tired as dogs, and mean, just mean. Tomorrow. When they'd rested up.

But what about now?

Well, there was this other friend of Ezra's that had sold that team to the sheriff and then wouldn't split the fifty he got. And Haze knew he got it because he saw that old fat windbag of a sheriff slip it to him. Two twenties and a ten. Hell of a friend *he* turned out to be, keeping all that money to himself.

But he was the best Haze could think of; only when he got to the Bar X, nobody was at home. House dark. Not even a dog to bark. It was spooky. But both horses insisted on water, and out of long habit he watered them at Buck Buchert's tank.

They were hungry, too. This was a mean sort of a

place, but after he had tied the horses he found some oats in a bin. He filled a half-bushel measure and made two piles of oats on the ground. He slipped the bits of both horses and let them feed, while he rested and thought things over.

Now and then he cried a little, like a lost child with a baritone voice.

What he needed was a drink and something to eat. He tied the horses after they had finished the oats. He like to jumped out of his boots when Ezra's horse turned suddenly and bumped Ezra's body into him. Haze heard Ezra make a kind of a belching noise, something he wouldn't've thought possible if he hadn't heard it. Talk about spooky.

Leaving the horses tied, he tried the back door. It was unlocked, but when he went inside he could not find one drop of anything to drink, and not much to eat. There was a skillet with some cold beans in it. He found a spoon by fumbling in the dark, and ate ravenously.

He was afraid to strike a match. Again he cried a little as he groped the kitchen, because there was not a bite of anything else to eat that he could find.

Suddenly he remembered the woman with the unfinished well. Say! He wished he hadn't got gay with her, but he sure had no such thoughts now. No, sir, all he wanted was something to eat. It had been *so* long since he had et. He was ready to bet that she was a kind woman underneath, and even if he had to eat at gunpoint it was better than starving to death.

He left the door open as he went out and it served them right for having such a sorry little old shanty with nothing to eat in it. It would serve them right if he set fire to it, but that would only get him into more trouble and he was already in enough.

There was a kind of a smell to Ezra, and he either belched or broke wind when the horses broke into a trot and shook him up. Haze sweat all over, but he had to have Ezra's body to prove that he had not even wounded anybody. But Christ, he hoped the son of a bitch didn't start to stink before he could turn him over to somebody else.

Straight as a die he went to the Four Plus. He judged it was getting on toward four in the morning when the house came in sight. He had seen a few stray cattle along the road, but not a single horse. Everything serene, but he wondered how he was going to approach that place without getting his hind end shot off by that woman.

He left the road, Ezra's horse with Ezra's body lashed across the saddle following unwillingly, tied by Haze's own rope to his saddle horn. Doubts and fears weakened Haze again as he came closer to the house in the darkness, and he licked his lips until his tongue was as dry as they were, and now and then he cried a little. He had never let anyone else see him crying, ever. But it didn't matter when a man was alone, did it?

He was a hundred yards from the house when he decided to explore the rest of the way on foot. He dismounted and tied both horses securely to a pair of trees, and went forward. There was a little light in the sky now —not much, but enough for him to make out the profile of the house and of that mound of dirt in the back yard. Have to be careful not to blunder into that well in the dark and—

A big-jawed, lonesome, confused bastard of a dog came at him, baying and snarling, and he froze. It kept coming, and when it made its jump he drew his .45 and fired at it without thinking. A gun had never sounded so loud to him. Fit to wake the dead.

But again he had proof that his luck had turned, because the dog stopped baying in midair and tumbled into a pile of dead meat, shot through the brain. "Well, say!" Haze said to himself, with a slight giggle. "Say, that ain't bad shooting with a strange gun, now, is it?"

He holstered the gun and approached the house craftily. He let out a scream as another dog came at him, silently, from behind. It got hold of his upper arm as he went down. This one was a big, long-haired bastard of some kind that went right for his throat once Haze was thrown on the ground.

Haze got the gun out and shot twice before he dropped the woolly dog. It did some kicking and gurgling for a minute or two, but no question about it being dead.

It was when he stood up on rubbery legs that he heard a man's voice booming up out of nowhere like he was in a tunnel somewhere.

"Who's shooting? Help me! For God's sake, give me a hand before I drown down here. Help, help, help!"

"Who's there?" Haze replied. He walked a few timid, uncertain steps toward the unfinished well. "Hey down there!" he said shrilly.

"Who is that? Help me out," came the reply like an echo.

Haze forced himself to look down into the well. Both men spoke at once. Both men recognized each other at once. It took a minute or two for Dave to make Haze understand what had to be done.

"Let it down slow! Don't drop the Goddamn thing on

my head. It weighs a ton. You let me hear that ratchet click, now."

"It's clicking."

Down went the bucket. "Hyo!" Dave called, and Haze began reeling him up. The cool night air struck Dave's legs, which were wet to the hips, and started him shivering. He showed his teeth in a snarl and jumped at Haze, clutching him by the throat with both hands. Haze fell backward on the pile of soft dirt.

"You ignorant sons of bitches," Dave panted, "you really kicked over the beehive, didn't you? Every lawman in the country is looking for you. What the hell did you kill them people for? I ought to kill you. They was my friends!"

He stopped banging Haze's head into the soft dirt and yanked him to his feet. "Then why," said Haze, "did you tell us to rob them? If you'd give us our share of that fifty, it wouldn't've happened. We'd've been long gone."

"You wasn't entitled to none of that, and I only told you where you could pick up a few easy dollars, that's all."

"You said they had a passel of gold pieces hid away."

"But Jesus, torture them to death! I got to live here. That old sheriff knows I know you."

Dave did not see the body tied across the horse until then. He gave a whoop of superstitious horror and jumped back. "What in *the-e* hell is that?" he screeched.

"That's Ezra Tully. I brung him back to prove I didn't shoot nobody. I didn't have nothing to do with killing them people, Mr. Conn, and I didn't kill Ezra. He flopped over dead of a heart failure. You can see for yourself."

"You hauled a dead body back instead of making dust for Canada?"

"I'll prove it. They ain't a mark on him, and you can see for yourself."

Haze shambled toward the tired horses that stood hip-shot, all-in, where he had dropped their reins. The full horror of the situation, the unbelievable depth and breadth and scope and effect of Haze's stupidity, hit Dave with stunning force. He had no gun on him or he would have pulled it and shot Haze in the back.

Instead he jumped him, his knees in the small of Haze's back, his hands on Haze's shoulders. Down they went again, Haze weeping, Dave strangling on his rage. He pounded Haze twice in the stomach to knock the breath and the fight out of him.

He then snatched out Haze's gun and shot him with it, putting the muzzle just above Haze's nose and blowing most of the top of his head off. Dave's teeth began chattering from a combination of cold and nerves. The first thing to do was put on his socks and boots. He put them on and then pounded at the kitchen door.

No answer. He was fairly sure that if Esther had been home, she would be pumping a twenty-gauge charge of buckshot through the door about now. He tried the door and found it locked, and then saw the padlock that Esther had snapped in the hasp just before leaving.

He wasted another of Haze's bullets, shooting the lock off, and went inside. He raged through the house, throwing doors open and leaving them open. He overturned the kitchen table and smashed a sad-iron through Esther's kitchen mirror just to make himself feel better. It did not help much.

He had to get out of here, that much was clear. He did not have to take out his wallet to know what was in it. He had exactly $305 to show for two wasted years of his life, for all that endless slavery for that babbling old nincompoop of a Buck Buchert. He was leaving a fortune behind, but it had to be done.

Esther and that son of a bitching kid had forgotten about his horse. He took the rope from his saddle, which hung on the corral fence, and caught the worthless stupid stubborn Bar X bastard, and saddled him. He took the .45 in its holster from the saddle horn and buckled it about him and then had to go back and search the bodies of Haze and Ezra for more cartridges. Between them they had ten.

It was broad daylight when he headed north, toward the Bar X. Old Buck would have some money around. He better have. Usually he kept some in a heavy brown envelope that sunflower seeds had come in, behind the motto in his bedroom that said GOD BLESS OUR HOME. He did not know that Dave knew about it; but he did.

The envelope was there, all right—on the floor, and empty. He saw where Haze had fed the horses and ransacked the place for something to eat. So far as Dave could tell, the fool had not omitted one single thing that he could do wrong. He might as well have left a note, "Dave Conn was the friend that told us about Paul and Reva Trotter."

Which was *not* true. Overcome with despair, Dave sat for a moment in one of Buck's chairs and buried his face in his arms on the table. "Esther," he whispered explosively. "Oh, Esther, I done my best for you but I had bad luck, I always have had bad luck, God knows I try and try and try, but oh God, Esther, I just can't seem to hit nothing."

He had *not* cheated Haze and Ezra; that fifty was his. He had *not* told them to torture Paul and Reva to death, just put a gun under Paul's nose and tell him to deliver. He had *not even dreamed* that those two miserable saddle bums could do a thing like that. How was he to blame?

But he would be blamed, all right. He would be hanged if they caught him. Not a thing in the house to eat, and he was a long way from Canada on an empty belly. But it was time to pull himself together and get going.

Get rid of this Bar X horse somewhere and pick up another one and then swap it some night for still another one. Long time since he had been a fugitive, and he hated it, oh God how he hated it. Since Esther Butterworth he had thought that all that was behind him. But he reckoned not.

CHAPTER SEVENTEEN

Grayson Figg had been out all night on what he liked to think of, secretly, as an *accouchement*. He had never been to medical school but he knew he had read all the books more carefully than most doctors who had. He had studied, really studied. He had asked questions, and the Lord knew he had had enough practice.

They would call him "Doc" only half in jest, and he had to take it. He had to do the embalming, which he detested, because there was no one else who was capable of it. He knew the nasty joke that went around about him —not maliciously but it might as well have been: "Well, Doc's all right, yes he is, especially if you're already dead."

This accouchement had gone well. Big, strapping girl of eighteen, first child and a nine-pounder if he was any judge, and he was. He was sure many a doctor would have started cutting and seizing with forceps, and giving morphine pills when she started to holler. But he had just sat there drinking coffee with the husband and, whenever a pain made her scream, he did not even turn around.

"Get up and walk," he said. "More walking you do, the faster it'll come."

"I can't walk. I bet I walked five hundred miles since I first came to you."

That was his prescription for the expectant mother—

plenty of liver, plenty of fresh milk, and walk three miles a day. Five was better, ten better still. This one had gone out in her fourth month to walk behind a team pulling the harrow for eight or ten hours a day.

Best thing she could have done. He delivered her of a fine big girl and stood over the husband while he washed it and powdered it and dressed it and put it in her arms. "You done this to her, Floyd," he said, "and my belief is that you shared the fun, you can share the work too. Your little old playhouse is spoiled for a few weeks anyway, and you ain't going to be making any new ones, so learn to take care of what you've got."

He was content to slouch in the buggy and let reliable old Mamie take him home. Grunt, the retriever (or he looked as much like a retriever as anything else), ran along under the buggy and kept a sharp eye and nose out for dangerous predators. Anything bigger than a prairie dog and Grunt wanted up in the buggy too.

It was Grunt who took alarm at the Widow Butterworth's open front door, flapping in the morning breeze. Grunt did not like anything abnormal, and Figg did not like something as abnormal as this. He always carried a shotgun in the buggy in case he got a chance to bring home a mess of prairie chickens.

"Ho, Mamie," he said, hauling the mare in. He got the shotgun out, made sure both barrels were loaded, and leaned it against the dashboard as he turned across the prairie toward Mrs. Butterworth's house. He again stopped the mare near the front door.

"Anybody home?" he shouted.

The open door kept on swinging lonesomely. He got out of the buggy with the shotgun in his hand and tied Mamie to the hitchpost. Not that she would run off, but at this time of day, after being out most of the night, she might walk off.

"Hey, anybody to home?" he called again, before going in the front door with the shotgun at the ready.

No one at home, no bodies, no bloodstains, and the only signs of violence were the overturned kitchen table and the smashed mirror. The back door was open, too.

The moment he opened it he saw the two worn-out, dejected horses and the two dead men. He had lived in this country long enough to take precautions in a situation like this. He cocked both barrels and toured the whole place before returning to the dead men, assured that he was alone, that no one would slip up behind him and drill him with a gun.

The one dead man had no wounds that Doc Figg could see. He had been dead long enough for *rigor mortis* to have set in, and when Doc untied the ropes and let him fall, he retained the curved position he had occupied while draped and tied across the horse. Doc was willing to bet that if he cut into his thoracic cavity he'd find either an embolism or a thrombosis, with a resultant infarction. Didn't look like apoplexy. No facial distortion.

No question how the other one had died. Both anterior lobes a mess, and the impact of the bullet making its exit wound had taken off half the skull, exposing the posterior lobes.

"Point-blank range," Doc said aloud. "And if you two ain't the ones that murdered Paul and Reva, I'm the big fat Mayor of Buffalo and a Democrat. Which I ain't either one."

One look down the well showed him water at the bottom. Water had been only a hope, a rumor, last time he heard Mrs. Butterworth's well discussed. He did not know what had happened here, but there were big, bare footprints all through that soft dirt. So someone had come up out of that well, just him and these two dead men—and everybody knew that Dave Conn had been shining up to Mrs. Butterworth by digging her a well.

One thing was sure, this was no place for him. He ran around the house and threw Grunt into the buggy. He untied Mamie, got in and turned her, and took the whip out of the whip socket for the first time in months. He laid it across her back until he got her running, taking the *left* fork—the one that led to Alec Pitman's Broken T rather than Buck Buchert's Bar X.

As soon as the mare got over her pique, she settled down to an easy lope. It was broad daylight when he reached the Broken T, but Alec had let his crew sleep in after their long chase yesterday and not much was doing. Buck Buchert was helping Alec do the morning chores, whistling as he worked. A well-dressed man that Doc had seen in town just a night or two ago was watering a saddled and bridled horse at the trough.

Nobody kept a neater place than Alec, nobody. Nobody cooked better than Edie, only usually she let Duke Palmer get breakfast for the crew. This morning he could hear Edie in the kitchen, singing away in that true, glorious mezzo-soprano voice of hers. Doc knew she was a mezzo whether anyone else in the county even knew what a mezzo was, but it was not something he would have called her without a chance to explain it to Alec first.

When I weep for the burdens I've carried,
   When I shrink from defeat, pain and loss,
When in shame and in fear I have tarried,
   Then I kneel for relief at the Cross.

Made a nice picture, the way she sang it. Doc heartily wished he could have her faith.

Alec introduced the stranger as Mr. Devlin, without explaining him. Mose Henry came stumbling out of the bunkhouse, aching in every joint and bleary for sleep and more sleep, as Doc told his tale. It was pretty hard to stagger Alec Pitman. He seemed to be prepared for just about anything.

"How long would you say since that fella was shot, Doc? Give me a time on it," he said.

"He was still warm. I happened into the place no more than an hour, at the most, after he was killed."

"Not much question in my mind but what it was Dave Conn."

"It was Dave's tracks, you can bet on that. You can see where he barefooted over to where his boots stood by the kitchen door. Now, to me that adds up to a well digger who had hit water the day before and had himself a place picked out to keep his boots."

Alec rubbed his chin. "No sign of Mrs. Butterworth or a rawboned kid of about thirteen or fourteen?"

"No, but her saddle horse was gone. And Dave's tracks was on top of the tracks of the other two horses. And fresher."

"You'd make quite a scout for the Army," Alec said with a little smile. "He'd go home first, to Buck's place, I'd judge."

"Sure. That's why I didn't go there."

"But there'd be nothing to keep him there, that's sure. He wouldn't head south, not on one of Buck's horses. And he sure wouldn't be caught anywheres near the Trotter place. You know what my guess is? The freight road to Lusk and then Newcastle and then the Black Hills. I don't think he knows that country." Alec put his fingers in his mouth and pealed an earsplitting whistle. "Buck! Hey, Buck, come over here, will you?"

Buck put his pitchfork down and came prancing over, gay as a kid. "Now what?" he said, his expression changing when he saw theirs.

"Buck," said Alec, "how much do you want, cash money, for Little Si?"

"Oh hell, Alec, I couldn't sell Si! If you want to use him awhile, or stand a couple of your mares to him—"

"I want to run his tail off. If there's one horse in the world that can do this job, it's him, and I don't expect you to stand treat. Will five hundred cash make him my horse?"

Buck looked as though he wanted to cry, but he needed five hundred dollars or any part thereof, and he did not want to shirk his duty. "Sure," he said. "If you need him that bad, he's yours."

"All right," Alec said, "go in and tell Ma I said to pay you five hundred dollars. Mose, you turn the boys out and get them fed and mounted up, and take the old freight road north. Doc, you come in with me and have breakfast while I have old Duke wrap me up some kind of dirty lunch to take along. He'll wrap your sandwiches in a suit of dirty underwear if you don't watch him."

"I think I'll go with you," said Devlin.

"No, you won't do no such thing," Alec said firmly. "You go see Father Lagasse. I know what you want to see him about, and if he *does* know anything, you find that kid. There'll be a mighty fine lady with him and I don't want either one of them scared. I want you to bring them back here to the house and keep them inside and safe. Are you armed?"

Devlin unbuttoned his coat to show a .38 belted high around his belly. "I've never had to fire it yet," he said, "but if I have to, I'll hit what I aim at, sir."

"I imagine you would," Alec said absently. "One other thing, Mr. Devlin. I ain't sure when I'll be back. But I want that boy here when I do, whether it's two hours from now or two weeks."

"We shall see."

Alec gripped Devlin by the shoulder. "We sure in hell shall see, right here on the Broken T. You and me is going to have a long talk when I get back. I'm asking you in a nice way. People around here generally try to accommodate anybody that asks nice. If you want to find your ass in the county jail, the sheriff is sleeping in one of my beds right now."

CHAPTER EIGHTEEN

He wished Little Si had been a bigger horse. No matter how good a little horse was, you could expect only so much of him. Like the old saying, a good *big* man is going to whip a good *little* man every time. Same way with horses.

The early-morning chill was not entirely gone from the air when he picked up the tracks of a good shod horse on the old freight road. The road had not been used much of late, and grass covered the bare earth that wheels had once kept naked and fallow. The brush that had been cut away, a little at a time, to let the wagons and coach pass through was beginning to encroach again.

Alec wished he had been a better tracker, just as he wished he had had time to learn so many other things. He thought he might have made a lawyer. He wished he had read more. He often wished he could play an instrument when he saw Ma struggling with that damn piano.

But there had never been any time for any of these things, just work, work, work until he was too old to learn anything. But he knew the tracks of a shod horse when he saw them, at least, and he could tell when it had been walking, trotting, cantering, or really burning up the dirt.

This one had been held to a nice, steady run, like somebody wanted to make all the time he could without killing the horse that bore him. Alec knew he was quite a way behind, but even if that was Dave up ahead and he was riding one of Little Si's get, it was not a horse that could go with its sire.

He stopped every now and then to let Si blow, usually where he saw tracks or other sign and it paid him to get down and try to read them. There never was much he could make out that he could not have seen from up in the saddle, but somehow the more he studied those tracks, the surer he was that it was Buck's old pardner-manager, Dave Conn, up ahead of him.

The road squirmed through a light stand of timber and forded a creek with a rocky bottom. Alec hit there shortly after noon. There was not much of a flow in the creek this time of year. He stopped and let Little Si drink a little, and then led him up the other bank. He knelt beside the tracks of the horse he was following and studied them.

They *looked* a little damp, as though they had not had time to dry out, and they *felt* a little damp compared to the dirt around them. If he was right about that, he was gaining. A man could talk himself into anything, of course, and one thing was sure, he was still a right smart behind.

Mose and the boys would be somewhere behind him, but not even close. He doubted that Max Maddox would be with them. Max had no reason to want to have to face Dave Conn down in front of folks, after paying him a buyer's commission of fifty dollars on that buggy team. No, if Max was smart, he'd decide that his official business was with those two bodies at Esther's back door.

On and on he rode. The sod had grown over the two wagon tracks for a long stretch, because this was sandy soil of open prairie, and easily penetrated by the rain that encouraged the spread of grass. Little Si's hoofs rattled the dried pods of buffalo peas, a sound Alec loved. He could just imagine how pretty it was here in the spring, when they were in bloom.

Another creek—and here he dismounted in a jump, full of excitement because there were boot tracks here, too. He held Si back while he tried to figure out what the hell Dave had been doing. It was there to be read, only he was like somebody who had never learned to read or write. Damned ignorant old cowman, he couldn't do anything right.

He led the stallion on and suddenly his heart gave a leap, and then he sobered and made sure his gun was ready. Here Dave had mounted up again, and now *his horse was limping*. The sign back there that had puzzled Alec was now clear to him. Dave had got down to pick up one of his horse's hind feet, perhaps to look for a stone in the frog, perhaps to feel of a tender spot in fetlock, hock, or leg.

A lame horse! That changed the odds, yes, sir, it sure did. Dave would be spitting tobacco juice into a whirlwind no matter what he did. If he pushed his horse too hard he might cripple him so he could not take a step. If he let him baby the bad foot or leg, he really would lose time. If he did what he should do—walk, and lead the horse—he might as well sit down and cry.

Alec carried a watch that his father had bought him secondhand, but he never had much occasion to look at it and mostly carried it just because he had got into the habit of winding it every evening. He took it out now, saw that it was three-twenty, and wondered how close that was to the real time. He had been through here before, of course, but not often, not enough to say he knew the road.

And it seemed to him that he had made a lot of miles

for the time he had been on the trail. Si was a tired horse, still dead-game but not bottomless. He *had* to catch up with Dave before darkness. It was a question of judgment and he had better be right when he decided it. Run Little Si's hind end off for a while? Or just keep plugging away, which?

One good, hard run might bring him up on a man with a crippled horse. Depended on how crippled the horse was. Take a small horse like Little Si, you could run him clear out of bottom if you asked too much of him. Son of a gun wouldn't quit on you. He'd just keep going until a foreleg gave way and down he went, with you going over his head.

Alec made up his mind. He'd make a run for it. Anything he did could be the wrong thing, but this was his decision.

He got up into the saddle and put Little Si into a canter and then, little by little, into a real run. You could tell by the way he bobbed his head, by the way he threw his feet down, that the stud was getting tired.

But up ahead stood a clump of trees, as good a place for an ambush as a man could ask for. Say Dave had to rest his crippled horse, and picked a shady spot. Say he was resting him there when he looked back and saw Alec coming on Little Si—why, there was cover enough to hide both him and the horse.

It was Little Si who warned him, Little Si who caught the breeze blowing softly from the north, carrying the familiar scent of a Bar X horse. He shot his ears forward and broke gait and Alec let him get away with it. Good quarter of a mile of deep grass between him and the trees.

If it was me, Alec thought, I'd tie my horse there and

slip back on my belly or hands and knees through the grass. Fight as dismounted cavalry, as my daddy used to say. . . . But he doubted that Dave had that much gumption. Dave didn't think very well. Dave liked being astraddle of a horse too well.

Little Si slipped into a comfortable walk. Alec stood up in the stirrups and shaded his eyes. Nothing to see, not a sign of either Dave or the horse, but Little Si knew! There was always a chance that Dave would have picked up a rifle somewhere, and if he had, why, Alec was in trouble.

But Buck Buchert did not own a rifle and Alec did not know anyone who had one that Dave would be able to borrow, especially in a hurry, especially if he had just climbed out of a lonesome old night at the bottom of a well. Because that was where he had spent it. How else had Doc Figg found damp tracks of bare feet in broad daylight?

He could size up pretty well how far a .45 would carry. He stopped just beyond that distance and stood up again in the stirrups.

"Dave," he shouted, as loud as he could shout it, "you want to come out with your hands up? Because I ain't going to fool around with you. If you don't, I'm coming in after you sure as hell."

No answer. No use fooling around. He turned Little Si and rode him back a couple of rods, to make it harder for Dave to break out and make a run for him in case he got the chance. He dropped the reins over the little stud's head and there he was, firmly ground-tied.

"All right," Alec called, "here I come."

A horse whickered peevishly in the shelter of those trees, and then did it again. It was the call of a horse that was glad to see a corral-mate. It was the friendly but respectful greeting of a gelding to a studhorse that never had been an abusive horse, but which could be any time it took the notion.

Alec could see the horse shifting around there where it was tied. One thing sure, Dave was nowhere near it or he would have shut it up. He was either to the right or to the left. Which? Well, you ran out of cover if you went more than a couple or three rods to Alec's left, and that wasn't good from Dave's point of view. That meant that he would be crouching in the brush somewhere to Alec's left, squatted down with a .45 in his hand.

Hell of a spot to be in.

He decided to head straight for the horse like a damn fool, and maybe bait Dave into behaving like a damn fool too. He called once again, "I warned you, Dave, I'm coming in after you," and then went in after him. Gooseberries and buckbrush and a lot of things Alec couldn't name. Perfect cover for a man afoot, just perfect.

He was less than fifty feet from the horse, holding his breath and itching all over, when he thought he heard something. He whirled to face the left with the gun outstretched, hammer back, both hands clutching the butt.

And just then Dave stood up with his own gun in his hand, but only *one* hand, so tired and confused and scared that he was afraid to shoot it out. The one time when he had a chance, when he should have come up pumping lead as fast as that gun could pump it, old Dave lacked the guts.

"Drop it, you son of a bitch," Alec said.

Maybe he should not have called Dave that name. Maybe that was where Dave got the nerve to try his luck.

Alec saw him make up his mind. Alec saw the grimace of rage cross his tired, haggard face, pulling his mouth down and narrowing his eyes.

Alec squeezed one off and saw where it thudded into Dave's chest, smack through his heart. Dave gave a sort of jerk as his knees buckled and he started to topple backward. He must have tightened up on his muscles some way because he fired his gun straight into the ground and then it dropped out of his hand and down he went.

Dead before he hit the ground. Well, Alec thought, I've often wondered what it would be like to have to kill a man. I reckon I still do. That toadstool there ain't rightly a man. And never was. . . .

The posse came up to him just before dark, sitting by his campfire and munching a sandwich. He had both horses tied out where they could graze. Dave's could travel but he was in no shape to carry Dave's body.

Sheriff Max Maddox, Alec noticed, was not with the posse. He had abdicated leadership to Mose Henry and Mose was bent double with the load of it.

"It's just a pulled muscle," Alec said, leaning over to rub the leg of the late Dave Conn's horse, "but he's a good one and we don't want to spoil him."

"That's sure the truth," Mose sighed, glad to have someone else making the decisions again. "No, sir, we don't want to spoil him."

"He can travel, but he can't pack Dave's body. We're going to have to tie Dave onto another horse and let somebody ride double."

Mose had his old personality back. "Oh hell's bells a'mighty," he foghorned, "why are you looking at me for? Why do I draw every privy-cleaning job on the damn place? I ain't going to ride double! Why don't we just drag him home on the end of a rope?"

"That's no way to talk," said Alec. "The son of a bitch is dead and a dead man is entitled to a little respect."

CHAPTER NINETEEN

It was the horses that gave them away. Mrs. Butterworth carried no rope on her saddle and Monte had had to tie them both with his rope, a hackamore at each end. Halfway between them he took a couple of half-hitches around a half-rotten log, but horses are adaptable creatures and these two had quickly learned to work together. When the kid came out of his dugout at daybreak, they were gone.

Just as he sighted them, halfway to the Trotter place, he saw two men riding toward him from the direction of St. Catherine's. It was impossible to mistake Father Lagasse, who wore a black cloak over his black clerical shirt and white clerical collar, and a flat black hat that made him look like a Spanish priest of the old school.

The second man he did not recognize until they were almost on him. There was no way to escape them so there was no sense trying to. He just waited.

"Hello, there, Spence," said the second man.

"Hello, Mr. Devil," the kid said sullenly.

The priest, a good rider on a cheap horse, dismounted but made no move to approach the kid. "We're not pursuing you, my boy," he said. "Surely the proof of that is that I've seen you before and I've left you alone, haven't I?"

"I suppose so," the kid said, since both men plainly were waiting for an answer.

"Why call him 'Mr. Devil?' That's not a very nice thing to say."

Mr. Devlin grinned. "He started calling me that when he learned to talk. It has been a friendly joke between us ever since. You look very fit, my boy."

As a matter of fact, the kid looked as though the sun had gone down on his world for the last time. As though fire and lava would start covering everything any second now.

"I'll catch your horses," the priest said, "and then I think you and I had better go with Mr. Devlin. He may have some excellent news for you."

"I'm sorry, I can't," the kid said, thinking of Mrs. Butterworth, whom he had to protect.

Well, *she* spoiled that by coming out into the open on the creek bank, where they could all see her. In a few minutes they were all mounted and headed for the Broken T, the kid carrying the shotgun he had left in his dugout the other day.

Even before they had tied their horses they could hear the chords crashing as Edie fought the piano to a standstill. Mrs. Butterworth's face got a look of wonder on it that made her about seventeen years old.

"A piano," she cried. "Oh dear, a piano, a real piano."

"Yes," said Devlin, "and a splendid one."

She was already gone at a dead run into the house, wearing a man's pants, with her hair a mess from having slept on the ground. She traced the sound of the piano to its special room, opened the door timidly, and looked at the beautiful, gray-haired woman who was struggling to master an octave plus one with her left hand.

Edie gave up. She beat the sides of her head with the

knuckles of both hands and wept. "Oh, God *damn!*" she said.

Esther ran to her side. "Use the A in the middle of the chord," she said. "It's even more harmonious that way. Look."

She tried to shape her hands to fit it, first the left and then the right. It was her turn to give up and cry.

"Like this?" said Edie.

"Oh yes, that's it, that's it!" Esther snatched at the sheet music. "Oh this is Mozart, isn't it? I never heard it before."

"Simplified Mozart, and I can't even play that."

"Try! Please, I want to hear it."

Edie could not resist that. She struggled through a few measures before giving up. "Oh, you've got the feel of it, oh that's wonderful, but your technique is so clumsy. Who is your teacher?"

"Him," said Edie, brandishing Professor Friedrich Schnabel's self-teacher at her.

"You mean you taught yourself to play *Mozart?*"

She pronounced it as though there were a *t* just before the *z*, and that was something new to Edie. There could be only one person able to pretend to that kind of knowledge.

"Say," said Edie, "you must be Mrs. Butterworth."

"Yes, and when I think of all the money my parents wasted on lessons for me, plus a piano, and I just am not a performer, I love music but my hands don't, and you—and you—oh, you're so *good!*"

They could only stare at each other. Then Edie said, reverently, "I'll be a son of a bitch," in a way that reminded Esther very much of Alec. Swearing like that took talent, the same as a piano.

"They say that those who can't, teach," said Esther. "I think I could teach you a lot, Mrs. Shook."

"Call me Edie," said Edie, who had made up her mind to shake Shook forever.

They did make progress at the piano that day. They went back to it again and again. They left the men to themselves. First the priest took the kid into a room and heard his confession and gave him the sacrament. Next, Devlin took the kid into another room and had a long, serious talk with him. In between times, the kid ate . . . and ate . . . and ate.

"That kid," said Duke Palmer, "is really something. It would be cheaper to feed your own ball team."

"Well," said Buck Buchert, "I haven't done badly myself, Duke. It's so long since I've had a decent meal! I'm haunted by thoughts of meals I'll never eat because I ain't got that much time left."

"Say, listen," said Duke, "I reckon you'll say it's none of my business, but I got a job to think about. What do you and Edie plan to do?"

Buck wrung his hands. "No matter what Alec thinks about it, we're a-going to move into my place. Edie vows to take some of this furniture with us. I just don't know what Alec's going to say."

"One thing," said Duke, "he'll need a cook if she leaves. Edie's learned me everything she knows, and a man can do anything better than a woman if she'd only give me a chanst."

Supper was long since over when Alec got back with the posse, with Dave Conn's body tied over somebody's saddle. He came around the back way to keep the hay barn between them and the house, so Edie would not have to see the body. Buck Buchert clamped his hat on his head and ran out, carrying a lantern in one hand and trying to put his mackinaw coat on with the other. It was getting nippy at night.

"Hidy, Buck. Where'd that old fat sheriff go to?" Alec asked him.

"He went to pick up them bodies, with Doc Figg," said Buck. "They neither one thought to take a lantern along to hang beside that open well. If somebody stumbles into it in the dark, Mrs. Butterworth could have a lawsuit on her hands. She wants to go do it but your ma said wait till you get home."

"Oh," said Alec, "is she here?"

That changed everything. It sure *did* change everything, he thought, as he and Buck walked toward the house—slowly, so Buck could get everything off his chest while his nerve lasted. Buck and Ma were going to take the sofa and the rocking chair and the piano, although Buck would have to build on a room for the damn piano first, and that would take money. Guess whose.

"The sheriff said you had told him you was going to buy that team and buggy from him," Buck said, "so she paid him for them, but she said we'd need a good team and buggy ourselves, her and me."

"Wait a minute," said Alec. "I don't reckon you and Ma aim to go over there and live in sin. You must plan to get married or something."

"Why, sure, what do you think?"

"I didn't know what to think. There goes my sofa, there goes my rocking chair, there goes my money to buy a team and buggy. And I did *not* promise that old fool to buy them."

"Oh, they're worth the price, Alec! Worth every cent of it."

"How much did Ma pay Max?"

"Two hundred and fifty. He wanted three."

Well, Ma was still Ma when it came to parting with a nickel. Suddenly he heard the piano clanging away. It stopped just as suddenly, began again, stopped, started.

"Esther," Buck said shyly, "is teaching your mother some playing tricks."

"Oh, does she know how to play?"

"Had eight years of lessons, she claims. It's Mozart they're playing."

Alec cocked his head. "I'd judge that Mozart has got a pretty good lead so far, if he can stand the pace."

Duke would have started in on him the minute he got inside the house, but Alec was in no mood to argue. "Rustle some grub to feed the crew," he snarled, knocking Duke's cards from the table. "I catch you playing solitaire once more when there's work to be done, I'll brand your ass."

"Supper's all ready," Duke snarled back, "and I don't have to take that kind of talk no more. What are you going to do for a cook when Edie leaves?"

It was something to think about, all right. Now he'd have to ride Duke's tail, too, plus all his other problems. Killing Dave Conn had not really bothered him until now, back in his own house. Here it was that he realized how many ugly, nasty, useless damn problems he had had all his life because nobody else seemed to give a damn. Like his daddy used to say, some pull, some just ride, and some ride and drag their feet. Hell.

Yet it all lit up like a new saloon when he and Buck went into the piano room, Buck proudly leading the way like he had some kind of a right to. That was Ma whanging away at the piano, back straight, head up, eyes locked into that music like a trapshooter following the spinning clay pigeon.

"Sh-h!" Esther said.

He went to stand beside her as she turned the music for Ma.

"There," Ma said, coming to the end of the piece, "I did it. It's the strangest feeling, as though I have not lived in vain." She looked up at Alec. "I reckon that's just a lot of beeswax to you."

He dropped his hand on her shoulder. "No, Ma, I honestly do know how you feel, and damned if I ain't proud of you. You do beat all."

It was as good a time as any to put his arm boldly around Esther and hug her to him. She made no pretense about being embarrassed. Snuggled right up to him. Looked at him like she could hardly wait.

While Ma and Esther set their table in the kitchen, while Duke fed the men in the dining room, he talked with Mr. Devlin and Father Lagasse and the kid and Buck in one of the front rooms. There just was no way to keep Buck out. He thought he was already family.

"You're not going to make up my mind for me," the kid said. "You can take me back but you can't make me stay. I'll run away again."

"If you'll just be quiet a moment, Spence," Mr. Devlin said, "I'm going to try to arrange for Mr. Pitman to take the responsibility for you. I think this is exactly the place for you, if you and he both agree."

"Fine with me," Alec said, anxious to get back to the kitchen and supper and Esther.

"This boy," said Mr. Devlin, "can be a real problem."

"He can get his butt whacked, too," said Alec.

"His father was Spencer William Holifield, Junior. I suppose you have heard of him."

"Can't say that I have."

"Shipbuilding and then railroad construction. This boy's name is really Spencer William Holifield the Third."

Alec grinned at the kid. "I like Monte better. I knowed he was some kind of a freak, but I didn't know it was that bad."

The kid grinned back.

"After his father died," Mr. Devlin went on, "his mother married again."

"Twice," Monte said.

"That's the trouble. Spence has failed—"

"Monte," the kid said.

"All right, Monte has failed in every school they put him in and frankly, his irresponsible mother doesn't take it seriously. Not all youngsters are good students—not all ever learn to be good managers of the kind of wealth that Spence—I mean Monte—will inherit someday. I don't think he will."

"He's the best damn horseman I ever saw," said Alec, "and I've saw a few in my time."

"Exactly. I think this is the place for him. Banks and trustees can manage estates, but how many men are as good at anything as you say Spence—I mean Monte—is at horsemanship? So if you will accept the responsibility for him, I'm going to recommend that his mother apply to the court to give you legal custody."

"What if she won't?"

"My firm represents the estate of her late husband. I don't think she can afford her present one if we exercise our right to reduce her income."

"I see."

Father Lagasse said, "The boy is a Catholic. I could consent to this arrangement only if he is brought up in that faith, Alec. I don't expect you to teach him his catechism, but I would expect you to see that he comes to church to learn it."

"He'll go," said Alec, "or he'll get a scab on his nose. All this, though, is up to him mostly, it seems to me. Let's hear what he thinks."

The boy tried to answer. Instead, he started to cry. He looked, out of habit, to the priest for guidance. Father Lagasse flipped his hand toward Alec.

"Go to him, my boy," he said. "I'll be your spiritual father, but there's the man who will raise you to manhood."

The kid flopped down and put his head in Alec's lap and bawled like a baby. All Alec could think to do was whack him on the back and say, "This is your home, Monte. You're at home, understand? Now let's go eat supper."

CHAPTER TWENTY

"But you're so tired," Edie said.

"Not that tired," said Alec, crossing his knife and fork neatly on his plate to show that he was full. "I'm uneasy about that open well, with no lantern over it."

"I'll go with you," said Esther. "I need to get out and get some air."

"Too much Mozart," said Edie.

Now, anybody was crazy to think that they could ride all the way down there to the Four Plus and ride back in one night, and Ma wasn't crazy. It was hard to think of old Buck being up to things like that, but him and Ma both was just too anxious to get rid of them. Maybe he had misjudged the old boy.

On fresh horses that would rather have stayed home, they rode at a gentle canter to the Four Plus. Most of the time they held hands. Now and then they pulled up to lean together and kiss. Alec tried to think how to tell her that he loved her and wanted to marry her if she'd have him. But Jesus, you didn't make a proposition like that to a widow-woman in the middle of the night! Not for anything would he have her think he took her lightly.

So he told her how he had planned to work the Broken T, the Bar X, and the Four Plus as one outfit. Find a good married man to put in Esther's house. Get in there with some crews and disk up that old wheatland next spring in time to sow grama grass and timothy before the rains came. If they got any rain next summer.

"Have I nothing to say about it?" Esther asked.

"Oh my lord, I done it again," he said dejectedly. "Ma says I'm highhanded and I reckon she's right. Don't you ever let me get into that habit with you."

"You won't, never fear."

He realized suddenly that they had crossed the bridge of marriage without his having asked her, and he still did not know how to handle that. They held hands again until they reached her place. When he lighted the lantern, its light told him that it was just twenty minutes to midnight. The very thought of the long hours still remaining before daylight almost choked him, but he *would not* hold her lightly just because she was a widow-woman.

Max Maddox had closed her doors for her. Alec found a stake that he could push into the soft dirt beside the well, to hang the lantern, while Esther held the horses. His hand shook.

He came back to her and put his arms around her and pulled her body hard against his. "God, I wish we was already married," he said into her hair.

"Why?" she whispered back.

"I wish I could say what I feel like saying without hurting your feelings."

"You mean," she said, "that once a cake is cut, you'll never miss a slice?"

"Esther! I said I wish we was *married!* I—I don't think that of you."

"Think what of me?"

"You will marry me, won't you? I'm out of my head, I love you so much. You ain't just been teasing me, now, have you?"

"Not as much as I mean to. Put the horses up and give me ten minutes. I'll light a candle."

"I—I mean get married, hon. Not just—"

"So do I mean get married, but I've been married and I'm human and I've been in love with you for a long time and you just ignored me. Now we have all the rest of the night to love each other. Tell me just one reason why not. Just one!"

Well, hell.